Welcome to the intensely emotional world of
USA TODAY bestselling author

Margaret Way

in her thrilling new duet

The Langdon Dynasty

*A family torn apart by betrayal,
brought together by love.*

In book one, follow Dev Langdon on his mission
to succeed his father as the Cattle King of Kooraki
Station and win back the heart of his childhood
sweetheart, Mel.
The Cattle King's Bride
April 2012

Watch for book two in The Langdon Dynasty duet:
Argentinian in the Outback

Read Ava Langdon's story of ignited passion and
love reawakening when she meets an exotic and
dangerously sexy Argentinian rancher.

Coming in May 2012.

Her heart gave a great lunge, its rhythm interrupted. For a moment, it was as if the whole world stood still.

"It's me, Mel. Let me in."

Shakers and movers would covet such a voice: beguiling and commanding at the same time. No way could she ignore him. No way would he give her the chance. Pulses racing, she hit the button to open the security door. She was on the top floor. The lift would deliver him to her in moments. Her feet sprouted wings and she ran down the hallway into the master bedroom. Her hair was wildly tumbled, there was a hectic blush in her olive-skinned cheeks, and her eyes seemed more brilliant than usual. She had changed out of her classic designer suit immediately after she'd arrived home, pulling a caftan over her head. No time to renew her lipstick. She ran a moist tongue over the full contours of her mouth.

As usual, he'd reduced her to a bundle of nerves. You'd think she would be well and truly over that. She who had gained a reputation for being cool, calm and collected. Only, she was hypersensitive to every last little thing about Dev Langdon.

MARGARET WAY

The Cattle King's Bride

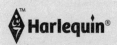

TORONTO NEW YORK LONDON
AMSTERDAM PARIS SYDNEY HAMBURG
STOCKHOLM ATHENS TOKYO MILAN MADRID
PRAGUE WARSAW BUDAPEST AUCKLAND

Recycling programs
for this product may
not exist in your area.

ISBN-13: 978-0-373-17799-8

THE CATTLE KING'S BRIDE

First North American Publication 2012

Margaret Way, a definite Leo, was born and raised in the subtropical river city of Brisbane, capital of Queensland, Australia, the Sunshine State. A conservatorium-trained pianist, teacher, accompanist and vocal coach, she found that her musical career came to an unexpected end when she took up writing—initially as a fun thing to do. She currently lives in a harborside apartment at beautiful Raby Bay, a thirty-minute drive from the state capital. She loves dining alfresco on her plant-filled balcony overlooking a translucent-green marina filled with all manner of pleasure craft—from motor cruisers costing millions of dollars and big, graceful yachts with carved masts standing tall against the cloudless blue sky, to little bay runabouts. No one and nothing is in a mad rush, and she finds the laid-back village atmosphere very conducive to her writing. With well over one hundred books to her credit, she still believes her best is yet to come.

Books by Margaret Way

MASTER OF THE OUTBACK
IN THE AUSTRALIAN BILLIONAIRE'S ARMS
HER OUTBACK COMMANDER
AUSTRALIA'S MAVERICK MILLIONAIRE

Other titles by this author available in ebook format.

CHAPTER ONE

AMELIA'S first call of the day was at 8:00 a.m., just as she was about to leave for work. The ear-splitting din of three phones ringing simultaneously, the main line, the extension and the fax, resounded through the apartment, shattering the morning's silence. Difficult to continue on one's way with that call to arms and pressed for time, she decided to ignore the triple summons. It would go to message and she would attend to it when she arrived home.

Her hand on the doorknob, something—call it a premonition—urged her to turn back. She felt in her bones that this wasn't going to be her usual day. Dropping her expensive handbag, she moved with care onto the white tiles of the kitchen floor—she was wearing stilettos—snatching up the phone.

"Mel here." Her usual engaging tones emerged a bit on the impatient side.

"Amelia, it's me," said the dulcet, slightly accented voice on the other end.

Anxiety settled in. "Mum! Is everything okay?" Cordless phone in hand, she dropped into a chair. The news wouldn't be good. Her mother wasn't given to phone calls. Mel was the one who did the calling and the emailing while her mother rang once a month. It was as though she had precious little free time. This early morning call had to be urgent. "It's Mr Langdon, isn't it?" Gregory Langdon, legendary cattle baron, was seventy-eight years old. His lifelong vigorous health had been failing rapidly over the past year.

"He's dying, Amelia." Sarina made no attempt to hide her powerful grief. "His doctor has given him a week at most. He wants you home."

Even given that kind of news, Amelia found herself bristling. *"Home?"* She gave a disbelieving snort, descending to a familiar dark place. "It was never a *home,* Mum. You were a domestic until Mr Langdon elevated you to housekeeper. I was always the housekeeper's cheeky kid. I've begged you over and over to come live with me, but you've chosen your own path." It was a tremendous hurt. She loved her mother. She earned an excellent salary; she was in a position to make life a whole lot better for them both.

Sarina Norton answered in her near emotionless way. "As I must, Amelia. You must steer your own way in life. You don't need to be burdened with me. Mr Langdon was very good to us. He gave us shelter after your father was killed."

No one could deny that. Not even Mel, although over the years their long stay on Kooraki had been the source of endless humiliation, with her mother the butt of scurrilous gossip. Her father, Mike Norton, the station foreman, had been killed in a cattle stampede when she was six. It had been regarded as a huge tragedy by everyone on the station. Mike Norton, the consummate horseman, had been thrown from his horse and trampled before his fellow stockmen were able to bring the bellowing, stampeding mob under control.

Such a terrible way to die. She had suffered nightmares for years and years, often waking with her own screams ringing in her ears. "Was that really so extraordinarily generous for a man of Mr Langdon's wealth to be good to us? He could have given you, a grieving widow with a small child, enough money to comfortably tide you over, before helping you get back to one of the cities. God knows Mrs Langdon hated us.

How did you tolerate that? I *never* did. Even as a child I used to rage at her. How could I not? The imperious Mistress of Kooraki Station took such pleasure in goading and humiliating you. Mrs Langdon hated us until the day she died."

"She hated us because Gregory loved us. You were a great favourite of Gregory's."

Amelia reacted. "*Gregory?* What's happened to the so-respectful Mr Langdon?"

Her mother remained silent. Her mother had long since turned silence into an art form.

Only silence wasn't Mel's thing. She liked everything and everyone up front. No secrets, no evasions. She had grown up with them hanging over her like a dark, ominous cloud. "So we're supposed to owe *Gregory* love and gratitude forever and ever. Is that it, Mum? That's ruthless old Cattle King Gregory Langdon getting in touch with his feminine side? He couldn't control his dreadful Mireille. She must have made him a totally lousy wife."

"Whatever, he *married* her. He must have loved her at one time."

"Reality check here, Mum," Mel said cynically. "She was the heiress to the Devereaux fortune."

"And she was the mother of his son and heir," Sarina retorted with no change of tone. She showed none of the fire of her Italian heritage. "There was no chance of divorce in that family."

"More's the pity!" Mel lamented. "Surely divorce has to be preferable to allowing lives to be damaged. Everyone suffered in that family."

"Divorce wasn't an option, Amelia," Sarina, reared a devout Catholic—or so she claimed—repeated. "And, while we're on the subject, Gregory couldn't control his wife when he wasn't there. So I suggest you be fair. Gregory was an important man with huge responsibilities, many commitments.

Mrs Langdon may have always wanted us out of the way, but she never got her wish, did she?"

"Now that's a tricky one, Mum," Amelia answered grimly. "We both know plenty of people thought, even if they didn't dare say it to his face, you meant more to him than his own wife." Why not bring it out into the open? Mel thought defiantly. The gossip that had had to be endured had left its indelible mark on her. So much bad history! Shame had been part of her life on Kooraki. She had grown up doubting herself and her place in the world. Dev had once said during one of their famously heated exchanges that her emotional development had been impeded. Easy for him to talk. He had the Langdon-Devereaux name. What did she have?

She had never been able to ask her mother questions. If someone gave every indication they didn't want questions raised, you never did. Even a fatherless daughter left in the dark. Yet she loved her mother regardless and had been fiercely protective of her all her life. Sarina, not that far off fifty and looking nowhere near it, was a very beautiful woman. What must she have been like in her twenties?

Pretty much like you.

"*We* meant more to him, Amelia," Sarina said. "Mr Langdon loved children. You were so full of life, so intelligent. He liked that. You were never afraid of him."

"Or of Mireille. I'm the definitive Leo, Mum. Surfeit of pride."

"I do know that, Amelia. You have to remember it was Langdon money that put you through school, then university."

"Maybe *Gregory* felt a tad guilty. Neither of us ever knew what exactly happened the day of the stampede. My father, from all accounts, was an exceptional horseman, an expert cattle handler. Yet he was thrown. For all we know, wicked old Mireille could have paid someone to spook the cattle and target Dad. Ever think of that? She was one ruthless woman.

She even went so far as to imply it could have been a David and Bathsheba situation, casting guilt on her own unfaithful husband. She was just so hateful."

There was another moment of utter silence as if her controlled mother had been caught off guard. "Amelia, I can't talk about it," Sarina said in a sealed off voice. "It's all in the past."

Mel inhaled a sharp breath. Her mother was in denial about so many things. She had long since faced the fact she only knew the parts of her mother Sarina was prepared to share. "The past is never dead, Mum. It follows us around. I *hated* taking Langdon charity."

"You've made that perfectly plain, Amelia. But you did take it. Please remember, beggars can't be choosers. Michael left me with very little. He hadn't been promoted to foreman long."

"Plenty of people told me what a great guy Dad was. I do remember him, Mum. I'll mourn him until the day I die. My dad!" She spoke strongly as though her claim was being contested.

"Do you think *I* don't miss him, Amelia?" her mother retorted, curiously dispassionate. "After I lost him I had to face the fact I had few employment skills. More significantly, I had a small child to bring up. I had to take what was offered. I'm glad I did, for all I suffered."

"For all *we* suffered, Mum. Don't leave me out. I don't know what would have happened if I hadn't been sent away to boarding school."

"Then please remember it was Mr Langdon who insisted you have a first-class education. You were *very* bright."

"I remember the way Dad used to read to me," Mel said with intense nostalgia. "Thinking back, I realise he was a born scholar in the true sense of the word. He craved knowledge. He was an admirable man."

"Yes, he was, Amelia," her mother agreed. "He had great plans for you, but I have to remind you, you wouldn't be where you are today without Gregory Langdon. Why, you were given access to one of the finest private libraries in the country right here on Kooraki."

"And wasn't dear Mireille savage about that?" Amelia did her own bit of reminding. Yet she had to consider the magnanimity of the gesture! A young girl, daughter of a servant, granted access to a magnificent library with wonderful books bound in gold-tooled leather with gilt-edged pages—the great books of the world, tomes on history, literature, poetry, architecture, the arts of the world. It was a library that had come together over generations of book-lovers and collectors. "What a cruel woman she was, poisoning every relationship. She even distanced her own son from his father. No wonder the grandson took off, but he never did say why."

"Dev, unlike his father, resisted control," Sarina said. "Gregory was a mountain of a man."

"That's not it, Mum," Mel flatly contradicted. "It was something more. Another unsolved mystery. Dev had to have had some private issue with his grandfather he wasn't prepared to talk about. Not surprising, really. They were one screwed up family."

"Too much goes on in your head, Amelia."

"Maybe, but I spent much of my life walking through a minefield. Right now I'm making a life for myself, Mum. I can't come—I'm sorry. I have a good job. I want to hold on to it. Mr Langdon may say he wants me, but no way the clan will. Dev mightn't turn up, either."

"I think otherwise," Sarina replied, quite strongly for her. "Ava and her husband are already here. Ava's marriage wouldn't appear to be a happy one, though she would never confide in *me*. Luke Selwyn is charming, but perhaps Ava isn't the woman he thought she was."

Mel reacted to the definite note of malice. "Please don't criticise Ava, Mum. Ava is a gentle, sensitive soul. In her own way she's had a tough time. Women have always been second-class citizens to Gregory Langdon. Sons matter, grandsons matter. Men are the natural born rulers of the world. If there's blame to be placed for a marriage breakdown it's on Luke. The charm—I certainly don't see it—is superficial at best. He's a shallow person, full of self-importance. He wasn't near good enough for Ava. Dev didn't like him and Dev is a good judge of his fellow man."

"But Ava *would* have him," Sarina said, again without empathy.

"She needed an escape route." Mel understood Ava's underlying motivation.

"Be that as it may! Dev has been contacted. He'll come and he isn't a forgiving man."

"Why would he be?" Mel's heart gave a familiar twist at the very sound of his name. "But it's his grandfather. They're *family,* Mum. I'm not. I have no place there."

"It was the first thing Dev asked. 'Is Mel about to obey the summons?'"

"And I can just imagine how he said it! That's exactly what it is. A summons, never a request."

Her mother provided an answer of sorts. "Gregory Langdon lived his whole life as the heir to, then the inheritor of a great station. Orders come easily to men like that. They don't really know anything else. Money. Power. The rich are very different, my dear. Dev is very different."

"I *know* that. His world view is simple. *Born to rule.*"

"You must make the effort, Amelia." There was a steely note in Sarina's voice. "Surely you're due a vacation? It has to be a year since your trip to New York. You and Dev are needed here. There is that bond between you."

A bond that up until now couldn't be broken.

Two parts of a whole. Dev had said that. Dev wanted her there.

Jump, Mel, jump!

What Dev wanted, Dev got. He lived in her heart and in her brain. Indeed, he was part of her. She had always loved him. She couldn't *stop* loving him, no matter how hard she tried, or the relationships she had tried to make work because she knew at some subterranean level Dev was out of reach. Only his dominance over her was beyond her control. Fate was unavoidable, predestined, she thought. She missed Dev more than anyone could possibly imagine, even if it was *she* who constantly held out against him and the tantalizing talk of marriage. She was lost in a maze of doubts and misgivings and she couldn't get out.

She had never told her mother that Dev had been with her on a brief visit to New York. She felt that the older woman would have vented her strong disapproval. Her mother, though ultra-restrained in her manner, had a curiously implacable streak and a blackness of mood that seized her from time to time. Odd that she would disapprove of her and Dev, considering the endless rumours about Sarina and Gregory Langdon.

Her brain churning, Mel hung up at the conclusion of the call. There was no denying Gregory Langdon had shown her affection as a child. Probably the fight in her had intrigued him. Would Gregory Langdon reinstate his splendid grandson? She had the absolute certainty that he would. Underneath the tyrannical hand, Gregory Langdon had been proud of Dev, loving him as he had never loved his own son, Dev's father, Erik. Besides, Gregory really didn't have an option. It was an open secret that Erik Langdon would never be up to the job. No way could Erik step into his father's shoes.

Dev could. She *knew* it would be wise to stay away from Kooraki for her own peace of mind. Stay away from Dev.

Stay away from the on-off passionate love affair neither of
them seemed able to resolve. In Mel's view there were too
many powerful forces aligned against it.

Dev—James Devereaux Langdon—in all probability his
grandfather's heir.

Who was she?

That woman's daughter.

She would never escape the tag.

CHAPTER TWO

GETTING through the day was surprisingly difficult. Even her boss at Greshams, the merchant bank, Andrew Frazier, had asked if she had anything on her mind. Obviously he had noted her abstraction and she owed him an explanation. He was her mentor and a kind of father figure, and she found herself confiding that Gregory Langdon, national icon, was dying. Andy knew all about the Langdons. She didn't mention she had been summoned to Gregory Langdon's deathbed. Only Andy, being Andy, asked.

Since she had been recruited straight from university with an Honours degree in Economics, Andrew Frazier had come to learn a lot about what went on under Amelia Norton's smooth, confident and very hard-working exterior.

"I don't *want* to go, Andrew. Nothing good can come from my going back to Kooraki."

Andrew steepled his fingers, looking across at his protégée. "But Langdon has asked for you and your mother wants you there?"

"Yes," she admitted wryly.

"Isn't the grandson the guy you're in love with?" Andy questioned, concerned about her. Amelia Norton was a very clever young woman, a glowing Italianate beauty, with considerable business skills, but he knew beneath the surface she wasn't happy or fulfilled.

"I should never have told you that, Andy," she said, dipping her dark head.

"Just answer the question. This love affair has been on the boil for years!"

The light of irony came into Mel's beautiful dark eyes. "A bit like Scarlett and Rhett."

"So what's the stumbling block?"

"Lots of things, Andrew. I don't want to get mixed up with the Langdon-Devereaux clan. Most of them are shareholders in Langdon Enterprises. I had to break free of all that. I have to *stay* free. Peace of mind is very important to me."

"I think it comes down to your fear of being dominated, Mel. I gather young Langdon is a very forceful guy."

"It's in the chromosomes," Mel said. "Nothing and no one, least of all me, could change that."

"You have fears he could possibly turn into his grandfather at some later stage of life?"

"Dev is a real piece of work," Mel said in a low voice. "A force of nature. He's as tough as they come. He'll take on anyone, including his own grandfather. No one does that. Absolutely no one."

"But surely you told me the old man was a virtual tyrant?"

"He was. He dominated Dev's dad, Erik, completely. With all that money and power, people tend to turn into despots."

"Are you sure you're giving your Dev a chance?" Andrew asked, disconcerting her. "I would have thought the last man *you'd* want would be a wimp." Such a man would never be able to handle her, Andrew thought to himself. "I thought we'd agreed your upbringing on Kooraki has a lot to do with your mind-set. The late Mrs Langdon being so unkind, your mother made to feel like a servant in the worst Victorian times."

"How I hated it, Andy!" Mel said, tears actually coming to her eyes. *"Hated it,"* she repeated.

"Yet Gregory Langdon saw to it you and your mother were protected. You told me yourself he paid for your education."

"You sound like you think I should go, Andy." Mel blinked furiously.

"That's your decision."

"So many mixed emotions!" Mel sighed. "There are so many cross-currents in that family. It's like a seething cauldron. Even between Dev and me. The cause, of course, is the collective hostility towards my mother. And me as an extension. Ava, Dev's sister, is the real princess. She's lovely."

"She'll be there?"

"Of course." Mel nodded. "Ava loves people, even when they don't deserve it."

"You're due for your annual vacation, aren't you?" Andrew Frazier saw his protégée was in two minds and needed helping out

"There's the underwriting of the Saracen deal."

"Burgess can finish what little there's left of that. I sense you think you should go, Mel. Your mother's wish matters. So does Gregory Langdon's. You owe him that much."

Mel met her mentor's shrewd, kindly eyes. "I would have to go tomorrow, Andy. His doctors give him no more than a week."

"Then get yourself organized, Amelia," Frazier advised. "If Langdon dies and you aren't there, I don't think you will be able to forgive yourself in the future."

At first she couldn't believe anyone was buzzing her at ten-thirty at night. She almost didn't bother going to the intercom. Probably some teenagers having their little bit of fun. It wouldn't be the first time. Only whoever was pushing the button to her apartment wasn't going anywhere fast. She had almost finished packing and a couple of items of clothing still lay on her bed. Thrusting her lush fall of hair over her shoul-

ders, she walked down the hall to push a button. Immediately
she received a clear video shot of who was standing in the
entrance to her eight-unit block.

Her heart gave a great lunge, its rhythm interrupted. For
a moment it was as if the whole world stood still.

"It's me, Mel. Let me in."

Shakers and movers would covet such a voice, beguiling
and commanding at the same time. No way she could ignore
him. No way he would give her the chance. Pulses racing,
she hit the button to open the security door. She was on the
top floor. The lift would deliver him to her in moments. Her
feet sprouted wings and she ran down the hallway into the
master bedroom. Her hair was wildly tumbled; there was a
hectic blush in her olive-skinned cheeks, her eyes seemed
more brilliant than usual. She had changed out of her classic Armani suit immediately after she'd arrived home, pulling a Pucci-style kaftan over her head. No time to renew her
lipstick. She ran a moist tongue over the full contours of her
mouth.

As usual, he'd reduced her to a bundle of nerves. You'd
think she would be well and truly over that. She, who had
gained a reputation for being cool, calm and collected. Only
she was hypersensitive to every last little thing about Dev
Langdon. She drew a couple of deep breaths to counteract
the onset of nervous tension.

Fine black brows raised superciliously as she opened the
door. Dev didn't hesitate. He moved inside with his familiar
athletic grace, dropping an overnight bag to the floor, where
it fell with a thud. "Are you going to hug me or what?"

Dev did mockery better than anyone. "Hugs would be only
the start." She shut the door, staring pointedly at the expensive leather bag.

"Have to talk to you, Mel." He moved into the living room,

looking around appreciatively at the lovely, inviting interior. Mel had real style!

"About what?" She reacted sharply.

"Don't play the fool. You, of all people, it does not suit."

"So what are you doing here?" The worst of it was he looked marvellous. Tall, rangy, wide shoulders that emphasized the narrow expanse of his waist, lean hips, long legs. A shock of blond, thickly waving hair curled up at the collar of his denim bomber jacket. Jewels for eyes, a dazzling shade of aquamarine that glittered against the dark golden tan of his skin.

Here was a man sexy enough to take any woman by storm. "I'm here to pick you up, dear heart. Your mother contacted me. I've got Uncle Noel's Cessna. We leave first thing in the morning."

She leant heavily into sarcasm as her form of defence. "Are you proud of the way you give orders?" She ran a backward hand over her tumbled mane.

"Not proud of it at all," he said wryly. "It's inherited, I suppose."

"Not from your father."

He spun to face her. His chiselled features with his strong cheekbones had grown taut. "Enough about my dad."

"Let's move on to my mother," she countered. There were always shifts and starts, backing off, coming together, combustible electric currents, with her and Dev. Why not? They had serious unresolved issues between them.

"Try to keep focus, Mel," he said briskly. "My grandfather is dying. He wants to see you and me." He stood back so he could study her from head to toe. "You look beautiful, Mel," he said in a dark, caressing voice. "More beautiful every time I lay eyes on you. Which isn't often of late," he tacked on in an entirely different tone.

"I thought we'd agreed on time-out?"

He contradicted flatly, "*You're* the one who always insists on time-out. Just how much time-out do you want? You're so into your intensive search for identity, it's become an obsession. You'd better find yourself soon. Neither of us is getting any younger. Neither of us is able to jettison the other. I know *you've* tried."

"What about you?" she retorted hotly, falling into the trap. "Isn't Megan Kennedy still in the picture?" An image of that very glamorous brunette sprang to mind. "It's certainly a match the clan would approve."

"Except for a couple of strikes against it. One, I don't give a damn what the clan thinks. Two, although I like Megan—she's a fun girl and doesn't pretend otherwise—no chance I'm in love with her."

"But shouldn't we treat love as absolutely foolish, Dev? What's that saying? 'There is always some madness in love'?"

"Nietzsche." Dev came up with the name of the German philosopher. "He went on to say, 'But there is also always some reason in madness.'"

"Madness either way. Love fades, Dev. Other attributes have to come into play—friendship, shared backgrounds and beliefs, eligibility. Sex isn't the be-all and end-all."

Dev gave a sardonic laugh, his dazzling eyes whipping over her face and beautiful body beneath its thin silky covering. "*I* wouldn't marry a woman I didn't want in my bed. My kind of woman would have sole possession of my body, my heart and my soul. The trouble with you, Amelia, is you're not only at war with me, you're at war with yourself."

She didn't reply. Her anger was *warring* with a terrible longing.

Dev threw up his elegant hands, callused on the fingertips. "Look, I don't want to continue along these lines, Mel. I could do with a drink. I need to unravel."

"What about a power nap, then take off?" she suggested,

hardly trusting her own voice. Whatever the friction, there was the never-ending thrill of his presence. "Where are you staying, anyway?"

"Mel, darling, I'm staying right here."

"Joke?"

"Can't say I'm full of humour at the moment," he confessed, stabbing a hand into his thick hair. It was one heck of an asset, that hair, Mel thought, bleached by a hot sun to a lighter gold than the last time she had seen him. "You can put me up, can't you, Mel? I'm not expecting to share your bed."

"Smart thinking, Dev. You *won't*." It was her classic defence mechanism.

Only he gave her a devastating grin. "Can't you say, 'I've missed you'? 'It's good to see you, Dev.' Something with a bit of weight to it?"

"Sorry." She shook her head. "You've taken me by surprise. And at this time of night! You could have rung."

"And have you hang up? No way! Drink, Mel. Single malt Scotch if you've got it."

She moved away, anxious to break eye contact. "So Noel lent you the Cessna?" Noel was the Devereaux patriarch. Dev, his great-nephew and godson, was the apple of his eye. Noel Devereaux had two daughters, but no son to succeed him. He adored his girls, both married to the *right* people, but it was a son he had longed for. Now he had Dev, since Dev had packed up and stormed off Kooraki. There was no love lost between Gregory Langdon and Noel Devereaux, both rich, powerful men.

"I do most of the flying these days. Noel is a good guy."

"It must be a big help having *you* around the place," she pointed out dryly. "Word is, you virtually run Westhaven."

"So?"

"So I thought congratulations might be in order?"

"I'm not an employee, sweetheart." Dev's tone was laconic. "I'm family. Uncle Noel actually wants to hand over control."

"You mean retire?" she asked in genuine surprise.

He shrugged. "Not exactly, but Diane wants to travel. She wants them to spend much more time together—see more of their girls and their grandchildren. The time appears to be right for Noel to hand over the reins."

"To you, obviously."

"The girls aren't interested, neither are the husbands, very successful city men. It's control, anyway, not ownership."

She didn't risk another comment. "Can I get you something else?" He had come a long way. And for *her*. Though it was as if she had little say in the matter.

"A ham sandwich, maybe? Could I grab a cup of black coffee, as well? You doing okay, Mel?"

"Wonderfully well, thank you, Dev." She maintained a cool control.

"So look at me. I always know when you're telling big fat lies."

"No lie. I'm highly regarded at Greshams." Mel began to assemble the makings of a ham, cheese and wholegrain mustard sandwich. The coffee would take only a few moments. "I'll feed you, then I wish you'd find yourself a hotel, Dev."

He pressed his back into the plush leather sofa with an exaggerated sigh of comfort. "Sorry, Amelia. I'm staying here. I need some sleep. Speaking of sleep, it's not too late for you to say you'll sleep with me."

"Get it straight, Dev. I *won't*." Mel's answer was remarkably breezy considering how she felt. She walked back, handing him a good measure of Glenfiddich over a few ice cubes.

He raised his remarkable eyes to her. "Many thanks, dear heart."

Knowing him so well, she observed, "You're upset."

He took a long gulp of whisky before replying. "Why

wouldn't I be? I owe him. *You* owe him. He cared about you. You were such a feisty little kid."

"So what went wrong, Dev?" she asked with some bitterness.

They were back on well-trodden ground. "We all know that," Dev gritted out.

"Your grandmother hated my mother and me."

His expression darkened. "She *feared* your mother. I'd say she had a certain respect for you, you little terror!"

"Well, she's gone now and soon your grandfather will join her. They'll lie together in the family plot, if nothing else. You're talking about running Westhaven. Surely you've considered your grandfather could have planned on handing Langdon Enterprises to you."

"After *our* bust-up?" he said, draining the rest of the Scotch. "Many harsh words were spoken."

"You've never told me what it was all about." She tried to fix his gaze but did not succeed.

How could he? Dev thought, leaning forward to place his crystal tumbler on the table, with its small collection of art books. Mel had more than enough to handle. Better he never told her. It was all so sick and sad.

"Okay, so you won't!" she said, her nerves frayed. "But, trust me on this, Dev. We both know your father has always found walking in your grandfather's shadow very heavy going. It's not in his nature or his area of expertise to step into Gregory's shoes."

Dev wasn't having any of it. "Dad will inherit as a matter of course," he said as though it were written in stone. "My father is the legitimate heir."

"Maybe, in the normal way, but your grandfather isn't going to allow his hard-won empire to fall apart. He needs someone to run it after he's gone. That someone is *you*."

Dev punched one fist into the other. "Dad has worked his butt off."

"I know."

Dev loved his mild-mannered father. He had always been very protective of him, even as a child. Erik Langdon was a long way from being incompetent, but it had proved impossible for him to emulate his dynamic father, a man with the Midas touch. Erik lacked the specific qualities it took to be the man at the very top of the chain. He had once gone on record as saying it was like trying to drive a vehicle uphill with the handbrake on. The Can-Do man had skipped a generation. It was Dev who had inherited all the skills necessary to succeed his tycoon grandfather.

"I'm sure your father will be justly rewarded," she said, as gently as she could, "but your grandfather won't cede him control. Want to bet I'm right?"

"Darling Mel, you *always* are," Dev drawled. "Let's get off the subject. Life is just one long series of hurdles for us."

"It happens when one gets caught up with wealthy, dysfunctional families." Mel matched him for sarcasm. "I'll get your sandwich. The coffee will only take a moment."

"You never intended to go, did you?"

She could have shown him her packing. Instead, she said, "I don't like letting my mother down."

"You've let *me* down, haven't you?" he flashed back. "How many times exactly have you told me you loved me?"

She took a deep breath. "I couldn't begin to count the number, Dev. But we live on two different levels. We have separate lives. You have an escape valve, being who you are. Soon you'll be the CEO of Langdon Enterprises, with huge responsibilities, always busy, always travelling thither and yon."

"Gimme a break, Mel!" His voice held a rasp. "You're a clever woman. You'd fit in supremely well."

Her laugh was raw. "Not with the clan, I wouldn't. They do have a hold on you, Dev. A few of them are major shareholders."

"So what? I can't solve your problems, Mel. Problems are keeping this God-awful distance between us," he said with intense frustration. "This damned love torment. The never-ending family stuff is the prime cause of our alienation."

"It's *your* family, Dev. Not mine. Such as it is. We've talked and we've walked all around our feelings. We're on a merry-go-round and we can't jump off. Any thought of marriage has turned into an impossible dream."

Dev leapt to his feet, his aquamarine eyes blazing with anger and outrage. "You know why? Because you're always applying the brakes. Think I don't know you fear being dominated? As though it could happen! What you *really* want is to bend my will to yours. It's the war of the sexes, with you the man-hater. You said you wanted to stand on your own two feet. I've gone along with that."

"Standing on my own two feet is central to everything." Mel tried to defend herself.

"But I applaud it, Mel," he cried in utter exasperation. "That's what you can't seem to grasp. I'm proud of you and how clever you are. You'd be a big asset to Langdon Enterprises, if you ever left Greshams. Anyone would think we were in competition, the way you behave. I don't understand what it is you want me to be. I can't grapple with all your expectations of the perfect man. I'm *me*. Far from perfect. Sometimes I think you're actually frightened of me. Not in a physical sense. You know I would never hurt you. But you do have this huge problem with male domination."

God knew it was true. "I grew up with it, didn't I, this little satellite orbiting a giant tyrannical figure. Your grandfather carried domination to the extreme. Always the iron fist."

"For goodness' sake, Mel," Dev protested, "he was *himself*. Stronger, cleverer, tougher than anyone else."

"You might be describing yourself." Mel shook her head bleakly.

Dev showed his fast-rising temper. "Now you're making me really angry. What is it you want me to be, Mel? Do you even know? I can't figure it out and I've come at it from every angle. As far as I can see, your biggest problem is *you*. Your exaggerated need for independence, self-reliance, like you don't need a man, as though a man could break you. I'm telling you it's paranoia!"

"Okay, maybe it is!" Pressure was expanding inside her, building up a huge head of steam. There were always bottled-up forces ready to explode when they came together, a consequence of their shared troubled history and her mother's illicit position in Gregory Langdon's life. "Let's stop now, Dev," she said more quietly. "I don't want to argue with you."

He sat down again, bending his blond head almost to his knees. "And I don't want to argue with you. But you are one strange woman, Mel."

"I expect I am," she said in a haunted voice. "You know your place in the world, Dev. All *I* know is I grew up without a father and a father's love and wisdom. What I know about my mother wouldn't fill half a page in a child's exercise book. She's the only child of Italian parents, Francis and Adriana Cavallaro, who migrated to Australia and settled in Sydney. It has a large Italian and Italian-descent population. There was no other family. My mother left home, a bit like Ava, to escape her father's very strict control. I never got to know *any* of my family. God knows why she decided to shift as far away as North Queensland. That's a long haul."

"Do we even know if that's *true*?" Dev muttered. "I wouldn't put it past your mother to have been wearing an impenetrable disguise all these years. When she came to

Kooraki no one would have questioned her background. Where she came from would have been considered irrelevant. She was simply Mike Norton's young wife."

"Terrible to think my mother's past could be an invention, a construct of lies. I hate blacked out spaces, secrets."

"Tell me about it," Dev said. "Most families have them. *You* are letting them plague you to death. You have to make a leap of faith. Faith in me. Your mother has her story but it's obvious she doesn't want you to know it, even if it would offer you comfort."

She gave him a despairing look. "Was her home life so bad she simply had to run away? Did she cast off her past like a snake sloughs off its skin? My dad would have known. But he's not around to tell me," she said with the deepest regret.

"One day your mother might confide in you, Mel." Dev tried to offer comfort, but he had no faith whatsoever in Sarina Norton, whom he knew as a devious woman and most likely an accomplished spinner of lies. "She's a secretive woman without your strengths. But she had no difficulty conning men into thinking they needed to protect her." He hadn't intended saying that. It just sprang out. His own view was that men needed protection from Sarina Norton.

"Con? Did you say con?" Mel asked, midway between wrath and shock.

"I did and that's my theory," Dev shot back unapologetically.

Mel was severely taken aback. Dev had never spoken harshly of her mother.

"Give it a bit of thought, Mel. Your mother is a born actress. If she'd made it to the big screen she would have won an award."

"What, playing the role of conning men?"

"I can't think of anyone better," Dev said bluntly. "Didn't

you ever watch her with the male staff? In fact any man that moved across her path."

Mel looked back at him, stunned. "What is this, Dev? Payback time? I didn't realize you so disliked my mother."

His expression hardened. "On the subject of your mother it pays to keep my mouth shut. I've never been out to hurt *you,* Mel."

Disturbing thoughts were sweeping into her mind. "But she thinks the world of you, Dev. How could you attack her, unless she tried to con *you?*" It didn't seem possible.

Dev picked a non-existent thread from his shirt. "Cons don't go down well with me, Mel."

"What sort of an answer is that?"

"Are we going to have a problem with it?" he asked in a decidedly edgy voice.

Not, she realized, unless she was prepared to launch into an all-out fight. "Did it help or *harm* her, do you suppose, the fact that she was so beautiful?" Mel asked, always looking for some way to unravel the mystery that was her mother.

"Hell, she still is." There was a harsh note in Dev's voice. "Beautiful women have a lot of power. You know that. You have to accept your mother's nature, Mel. I know you wanted her to come live with you, but the reality was she wanted to stay on Kooraki."

Mel responded with real grief. "She chose Kooraki over me. She chose your grandfather over me, a man old enough to be her father, but what the hell? He was anything but your average bloke." With a defeated sigh, she picked up the laden tray. Dev stood up to take it from her, setting it down on the coffee table.

She let him eat in peace. She had poured two coffees. Now she sat opposite him, sipping at hers, the rich aroma tantalizing her nostrils and soothing her.

"That was good!" he exclaimed in satisfaction when he

was finished. "I haven't had anything since around ten this morning."

"Why is Mum so set on my attending?"

"Why are you so set against it?"

"All your grandfather thinks he has to do is give the order and we all fall into line. Well, most of us do," she said wryly. "Not you, of course, even when you were told you were being cut out of his will."

"Big deal!" Dev exclaimed. "I was prepared to risk it. I never felt good about telling my grandfather to go to hell, Mel. It was just something that had to be said. And there's another thing. Whether he meant it or not, he broke Dad's spirit."

"I can't understand why your father never stood up to him."

Dev's brief laugh was without humour. "Not everyone is a born fire-eater, Mel. Besides, he had to contend with a double whammy. Between my grandfather and my grandmother, Dad had a rough ride. My mother tolerated the situation as long as she could before she had to take off. Self-preservation. I used to dream of her coming back. Poor Ava was the worst affected. But at least we see our mother now. The truly amazing thing is they're still married. Neither of them filed for divorce. Both could have found new partners in record time."

"I expect your grandfather forbade it."

"Maybe he did." Dev shrugged. "He might have stopped Dad, but not Mum. She broke free. My parents should have moved away from Kooraki after they were married. They should have had a home of their own. I remember they were happy once. I believe they still have strong feelings for one another."

Mel thought so, too. "Will your mother come?"

Dev nodded. "If Gregory dies, there'll be the funeral."

"Is Ava happy?" Mel asked. Lovely, graceful Ava, the granddaughter shoved into the background.

Dev gave a brotherly howl of anguish. "We both know Ava

chose marriage as a way out. She had no real idea of what she was letting herself in for. She always claims she's happy, but I don't accept that. If I ever found out that husband of hers was ill-treating her in any way—not physically. He wouldn't dare—but trying to browbeat her, he'd better look out. And that's a promise."

Mel had no doubts about that. She stood up. "For your information, I did intend to go, Dev. I'm as good as packed. I'll have to cancel my morning flight."

"Better do it now," he said, rising to his feet and carrying the tray back into the kitchen. "I'm not exactly sure where I'm to sleep. Obviously the master bedroom is *verboten.* No need to lock the door, by the way. I don't bother women."

"No. It's generally the other way around."

"I'm a man like any other, Mel." He gave her a sweeping glance out of his aquamarine eyes. "Even for you I can't swear off sex entirely." There was a sardonic twist to his handsome mouth.

"No need to tell me," she said with an acid edge. "Someone always manages to give me the latest gossip. I knew all about your little fling with Megan Kennedy."

"Megan knew what she was getting into," he said, unperturbed. "We're still friends."

She rounded on him, temper flashing. "Isn't that lovely!" She hadn't forgotten how fearfully upset she had been, how hard it had been to hide it. The "Megan" affair had been her worst case of jealousy yet. She had to remind herself she'd had her own little flings that were predestined to fail.

"Might I remind you the pot can't call the kettle black?" he said suavely. "Now, where do I sleep?"

She waved an imperious arm. "There's the second bedroom, as you well know. The bed is made up."

"You only have to call out if you get lonely, Mel."

"My head only has to touch the pillow and it's lights out," she assured him.

CHAPTER THREE

DESPITE her claim, Mel lay awake with the full moon casting its light across her bedroom. Maybe it was the coffee that was keeping her awake? That was the easy answer. The real answer? How could she sleep with Dev just down the hall? She knew what her problem was. She was sexually frustrated, assailed by desires she couldn't control with him around. She had to ask herself—could there possibly be another man in the world for her but James Devereaux Langdon?

Restlessly, she kicked at the top sheet, freeing her feet. She punched the pillows yet again, then turned on her left side, only she wasn't comfortable with the steady thud of her heart. Over to the right side, she checked the time. Twelve forty-five. She would be exhausted in the morning if she didn't succeed in putting Dev and her body's needs out of her mind. Ten minutes went by. Was there *no* way out of this? It was as though a tribal sorcerer had put a spell on her. There were one or two old sorcerers left on Kooraki. Magic and ritual with the Aboriginal people would never die out. Only she knew as well as anybody you couldn't get everything you wanted in this world. She had wanted a career. She had one. She had gained the respect of her peers and notice from the hierarchy. She was earning really good money.

You made a big mistake letting Dev stay.
He knew exactly how to push her buttons.

In the guest bedroom Dev was having an even worse time
of it, the area below his navel aflame. He was unbearably
aroused. He wanted to get up and go down the hall to her.
He gave a short frustrated laugh that he muffled against the
pillow. The last thing he should do was put Mel under even
more pressure, even if it was killing him keeping his hands
off her. Why was it he never had a problem with other women,
yet he had one big problem with Mel? He threw the top sheet
off, trying to rein in emotions so driving they threatened to
sweep away any misgivings. This constant pitch of desire he
had for Amelia could be classed as a type of lunacy.

His poor embattled grandmother had tried hard to con-
vince him that Mel could have been Gregory's daughter.
It had upset him enormously at the time, but he had never
really believed it. His gut told him not. And his gut was right.
It was a pathetic and cruel attempt on his grandmother's part
to separate him from Mel. Yet he had understood his grandmother's raging jealousy. His grandfather *had* lost his heart.
But not to his lawfully wedded wife. It was there in his grandfather's eyes every time he looked at Sarina.

He had no idea when that love had been consummated.
Perhaps after the tragic death of Mel's father. Mike Norton
had been a leading hand on Maru Downs, a North Queensland
station in the Langdon chain. His grandfather's normal practice was to visit all the stations and the outstations checking
on operations. There he had met Sarina, Mike Norton's beautiful young wife.

His grandfather had offered Mike a job on Kooraki. No
question Mike had been foreman material, well up to the job
offered, but the intense allure of Norton's young wife could
have been the deciding factor. Was that what had happened?

His grandfather had been a man of strong passions. Sexual passion had a way of not allowing its victims to escape.

He should know.

Afterwards, she told herself she didn't really remember walking down the corridor to Dev's room. Maybe her mind was playing tricks, surrendering to a dream. It was not as though they didn't know one another's body intimately, but the thrill, the rapture, the sense of belonging had never lessened, never lost its power.

Dev heard the door handle turn. He swung onto his back, looking up to see Mel framed in the doorway. There was enough light from the full moon to see her clearly. She was wearing a pale coloured nightgown that shimmered like moonbeams.

He sat up, startled, supporting himself on one elbow. "Are you okay?"

She shook her dark head.

"What is it, Mel?"

She gave a little laugh that sounded like a sob. "I'm never okay. You know that." She moved across the room, then sat on the side of his bed, staring into his eyes.

"You can't do this, Mel," he protested, his whole body powerfully, painfully aroused.

"I want to sleep with you," she said, dragging the top sheet away from him. It exposed his naked hard-muscled chest with its tracery of golden hair.

His voice held a tense warning. "You get into this bed and we're going to have sex, Mel," he said. "You *know* that. So don't try the little-sister routine."

"No, no. I come to you for comfort, like I always used to." She hesitated for a fraught moment, then said, "How long did we think we might be closely related, Dev?"

He exploded, just as she knew he would. "For half a second! Well, me, anyway. Always the eternal anguish, Mel, the eternal question. You'd go to any lengths to drive me mad. Do you *seriously* believe I would have ever touched you had I believed it? Are you that crazy?"

She shook her head in shame.

"Am I supposed to give you a round of applause for that?"

"Don't be like that, Dev," she begged. "There was so much gossip."

"Mireille's poison." His verdict was harsh. "She had a great talent for implying sinister, cruel lies. Jealousy is one of the most powerful deadly sins. It gets people murdered every day of the week."

"Poison finds its way into the bloodstream. My mother bewitched him."

Dev put his two hands to his head, groaning. "Okay, so she did! And hasn't there been a tremendous emotional fall-out?" Angry and immensely frustrated, he put strong hands on her, pulling her down and then into the bed beside him. "Are we going to continue this interminable conversation?" He hooked one strong arm around her. "You, woman, drive me mad. I just want to draw a secure circle around the two of us so no one can get in. God knows we've lived our lives with controlling people. Both of us have resented it bitterly. As a consequence, you're in retreat from me in case I turn into the biggest controller of them all."

Her laugh was woefully off-key. "Let's face it, being the man in control is going to be your role, Dev. You'll find that out when your grandfather's will is read. Most of the time I was able to separate the truth from the sick rumours. But I was just a little kid, Dev. My father was dead. Mum and I had no protection from that all-important quarter. My father wouldn't have stood for—"

"I find the whole issue unbearable, Mel. I worry about

you. You're so clever, so seemingly confident, a beautiful woman. Anyone would say you've had the lot, yet a crucial part of you remains a lost little girl. Fragile."

"I am *not!*" she protested, hitting a hand to his shoulder.

He caught her hand, kissed it. "Most people don't see it. I do. So my grandfather and your mother loved one another. Is there anything wrong with love? Love might be madness, but it's glorious, as well. Look at you and me. It takes a real man to put up with you. God knows my granddad didn't get unconditional love and affection from my grandmother. She was the ultimate possessive woman. It helped to be an heiress in her own right. Gregory was her paid-for possession. She did pump a lot of her own money into Kooraki during the lean times."

"Then he married her for her money?"

"Maybe he thought she was a lot more docile than she really was. He wouldn't be the first man to take a wealthy bride. He sure isn't going to be the last. Countless women marry for money, social position, security. Nothing much has changed from the old-style marriage of convenience. It still goes on. The odd thing is that a lot of the time it works better than the madly in love scenario. Like us."

Mel didn't argue. She had observed that among her circle of high-flying friends. "I suppose neither side has high expectations of the other," she offered in explanation.

"For the life of me, I couldn't do it," Dev said. "But I'm not going to spend the rest of my life tippy-toeing around you, Mel. You reckon I'm a tough guy, right?"

"Precisamente," she said. "You're already tycoonish."

"Tycoonish? Is there such a word? If there is, spare me!" he groaned. "A ruthless tycoon could have found a sure way to capture you. I could have made you mine. Made you pregnant. You would have had to marry me and not carry on with all the old-style, hopelessly outdated class distinctions."

"They'll never be outdated," she contradicted flatly. "It's human nature. God, Dev, I'd *love* to be pregnant," she cried. "My biological clock is ticking away. I want children. I love children. I want to hold our baby in my arms."

"Stop, oh, *stop!* I have a burning need to clarify this. You want *our* baby?"

"Of course I do."

"You mean I don't need to give up hope?" he shot back with extreme sarcasm.

"You know what they say—hope springs eternal."

"Quit the smart talk, Mel. I'm in no mood for it. You have a bizarre way of attaining your objectives. But then you probably deal in the larger concepts of life. I'm too busy."

"I know how hard you work," she said in a conciliatory tone.

"Can you tell me this? Are you planning on prolonging this sex-starved unmarried state for the foreseeable future?"

"It *is* exciting," she said, shivers running down her spine.

"Oh, yes. Unlike you, I don't consider it to be *cool.* You're using your beautiful body as a serious weapon, like right *now.* No, don't get angry." He placed a taut restraining arm across her breasts. "Think about it."

Mel loved the weight of his arm. She turned her head to stare up at him, the planes and angles of his dynamic face, the high sharp cheekbones, the width between the jaw bones that tapered to a strong chin with its distinctive Langdon cleft. "I can't *think* when I'm in bed with you."

"Who needs you to *think?*" He withdrew his arm. "It might be a wise move to go back to your own bed, Mel." He spoke in cool, sarcastic style. "What better thing is there to do in bed but sleep? It's all down to you. Go on. Get up."

"If I can."

"It's your practice to do what you damned well like. You're

free to walk away, Mel. I could point out there are plenty of women I know who wouldn't consider it."

"Tell me something I don't know," she said, still not moving. "I'm pretty hotly desired myself."

"I don't want to hear about it, thank you," he said in a flat, hard voice.

"I remember a time when you used to be nicer," she quavered. She didn't want to fight. Her need for him was fierce.

"God help me, don't I regret that now?" Dev suddenly lifted himself on his strong arms to loom over her. "You want me to make love to you, is that it, you crazy woman?"

Wasn't it her dread that she could drive him away with her fears and phobias? At one time she had seriously considered DNA testing, then backed off in shame. Gregory Langdon couldn't have been her father, although he had been on the scene. Mike Norton was her father. He had loved her. Could a man love a child he knew wasn't his? Maybe some men could. The child couldn't be blamed for the sins of the fathers.

"Well?" Dev growled.

She threw all her chaotic thoughts out of the window. "Yes, yes, yes, yes!" she cried. "A thousand times ye—"

He stopped her by lowering his body onto her, covering her, letting her feel his full weight—taut, hard body, the musculature, the rib cage so clearly defined the imprint was left on her body, her flesh satiny-soft and yielding to his potent maleness. His mouth came down near mercilessly on hers. But wasn't she starved for it, hot and aching with longing? She could never mistake Dev for anyone else, not even in the blackest night with her lack of vision total. Every part of her recognized and accepted him—the scent of him, the magical feel of him, her wild response. Her very flesh lit up in ecstasy for him. So did her heart, flowering in her chest.

Dev kissing her was the most ravishing feeling in the world. It was so intensely erotic, it transformed her not into an acquiescent, trembling creature, but a voluptuous woman. She cried out with pleasure. He was a masterful manipulator, but the mastery was inherent in everything he did. How could she relish the sexual excitement that came with the dominant male, then tell him perversely that she feared domination? She had to be a basket case.

Still kissing her, Dev moved off her, falling back onto his side. "You drive me mad with wanting you," he rasped. "I should really be thinking about going into therapy if I had the time. I could take up something calming like arts and crafts, maybe wood whittling."

"I'm sorry, Dev." She pressed close to his body, sighing and breathing into his ear.

His mouth clamped on hers. "Damn you, Mel." His hand slid a little roughly down the length of her abundant hair. "Just tell me what you want and I'll give it to you."

A shiny tear fell onto her cheek. *"You."*

"You want *me,* not *us?*"

"Just love me, please," she begged.

"But I want *us,* Mel! Be warned. There's a caveat attached to all this. I'm *not* going to wait for you forever." He spoke forcefully, even as he was trying to keep the immensity of his desire for her in check. There were still walls to be knocked down with Mel. Even as a child, Mel had felt impelled to rebel against Langdon authority. He knew his grandmother had been hateful to Sarina. Mel, too, but it was Mel's determined nature that made her fight back.

His great hope was his grandfather's passing would put an end to the chaos of the past with all its moral dilemmas. Mel's fears were born out of extremes. He understood her. He loved her. But it was hell. So much time and pain had passed between them. There had to be a resolution.

Her body gave off heat and its own intoxicating fragrance. He could feel the heat off her beautiful breasts and the heat between her legs. He rested his hand there. "Listen, I adore the nightgown, Mel, but it has to come off."

"Just *do* it," she begged, moving her body to make things easier for him.

"That's an irresistible plea if ever I heard one," he mocked. "Okay, let's try it inch by inch." He drew her nightgown slowly up the length of her legs, past her taut stomach, her narrow waist, letting the silk-satin lie in folds under her breasts. Then he moved down to the bottom of the queen-size bed—too small for a man like him—taking her elegant feet in his hands.

Mel lay back, eyes closed, in a state of surrender. Her short-term forays into other far less troubling relationships had brought home to her she would never be satisfied with any other man but Dev. No one else seemed to know what she wanted. No one else could cause the throbbing in her breasts, the mad flutter like a million butterflies in her stomach, the little electrical charges all over, the tiny, keen knife-like thrusts between her legs. No one else could even bring her to orgasm. She had never been able to fake it. Odd that lack had never been noticed.

Dev was kissing her bare feet. The lick of his tongue and his kisses moved languorously up her trembling, increasingly restless legs. He pressed his lips to her flat stomach, the tip of his tongue tracing the whorls of her navel, then his mouth began its downward trail again to where her body was pulsing white-hot. She could hear his breath deepening and quickening. Her own breath was shortening. With exquisite smoothness, his index finger glided inside her—she was *so* ready for him. Her heart leapt like a wild bird bouncing off the walls of its cage.

God! Oh, God! Oh, God!

"Please, Dev, come inside me." She knew she was whimpering. The muscular contractions were growing so strong, she felt she might climax too soon.

"Just you wait a bit longer," Dev murmured, clearly taunting her. "Punishment isn't over yet. I want you to come alive for *me,* no one else."

Her flesh had melted. Her bones had turned to liquid lava. This was what Dev wanted, as much sensation as possible. "Dev, my heart is ready to explode." She was feverishly turning her head from side to side. Her long legs had fallen apart of their own accord.

"Just a little longer," he murmured.

"You *devil!*"

"Whose fault is that? With you, I have to take my pleasure when I can."

Moments later, judging it precisely, he removed her nightgown with care, then threw it unerringly towards a chair, where it landed in a silky pool. Her breasts were uncovered to his gaze, her hyper-sensitive coral-pink nipples tightly budded and standing erect.

There was a roaring in Mel's ears as he took one, then the other, into his mouth.

"Tell me you love me," he muttered, determined on causing her at least some of the pain she caused him.

She didn't answer. Her total focus was on wrapping her legs strongly around him, tightening them. She wanted to capture him, not knowing when exactly he had managed it, but he was as naked as her. Their nakedness felt absolutely right. It had from the very first time. Dev was her first lover. He had taken far more than her virginity. He had taken her lifelong allegiance.

"You know I love you." Her body was breaking out in a fine dew of perspiration, the exquisite agony of want. "You've marked me forever."

"I'd say we marked each other," he said harshly, not at all satisfied with her answer. "Say it. You-*love*-me."

"I-*love*-you." She tried to lift her head off the pillow, her voice barely above a ragged whisper. "Oh, *please,* Dev." Her body, so long starved of him, was frantic for release. Yet he wanted to circle her like an eagle.

He bent his head to lick away the trail of her hot tears, then descended into kissing her, savouring the lush texture of her lips, tasting the nectar within. Only then did his strong hands move beneath her satiny heart-shaped rear, cupping it, then lifting her body high so its delta was close-up and ready. He wanted to bury himself deep, ever deeper inside her so they fused.

Her little keening cry was the trigger. He came in a flooding roar. She came with him in her own burst of fire.

He wouldn't have changed places with any other man in the world.

He had waited and *waited* for Amelia. It had made many aspects of his life excruciatingly difficult. What Mel had to learn now was he would never let go. The waiting was over. He would not stand for interference from anyone. That included Mel. The king was near death. Long live his successor.

Gregory Langdon lay very still in his magnificent brass-studded mahogany bed that had been custom made for him decades before. His skeletal hands rested on the coverlet. The heavy curtains Sarina had almost drawn shut blocked the glare of sunlight from outside. His son, Erik, was downstairs. Ava, Erik's daughter, his beautiful granddaughter, had arrived with her no-account husband. He guessed the cracks were already appearing in that ill-advised marriage. He and Ava had quarrelled over the young man she had only imagined she loved. On the surface, Luke Selwyn had appeared a suitable suitor for his granddaughter's hand. His family had money—so he wasn't a fortune-hunter but over a period of time Selwyn's less-attractive qualities had begun to surface. He was basically a lightweight, a *floater* through life, all drive and ambition blunted by wealth.

In the end Gregory had made it very plain that he was violently opposed to the marriage, but gentle, sensitive Ava for once in her life had defied him and ignored the concerns of her brother. Dev had been against the marriage, as well. Dev was devoted to his younger sister and her to him.

He knew the rest of them had arrived—Langdons and a fair sprinkling of Devereaux. They thought the world of Dev, nicknamed after *their* family. They looked up to Dev and admired him.

Only so far—and he couldn't hold out much longer—no Dev and no Amelia. He drew a shallow breath, pain sweeping over him in a monstrous wave. He was dying. He accepted it. There was no place else to go. The pain would finally cease. But he couldn't die before Dev and Amelia arrived. He had resisted another jab of the needle that lessened the agony but befuddled his mind. Even dying, he needed to be in possession of his faculties. The pain didn't matter. He needed reconciliation even if he didn't deserve it. Dying was a terrible business. Better to die quickly than have an agonizing end drawn out. He had been such a vigorous man. Splendid health he had taken for granted. But finally the traumas of old age had unleashed themselves upon him. Black oblivion would come as a mercy.

At a slight sound, Gregory Langdon looked towards the bedroom door. Probably the nurse. He didn't like her one bit. A big, broad-shouldered, no nonsense woman, competent, but distressingly plain. He was used to having beautiful women around the place—Ava, Amelia, and the light of his life, Sarina. There had been no happy start, let alone a happy ending for him and Sarina. That was one miracle he couldn't command. The timing, right from the beginning, had been all *wrong*. He and Sarina, a married woman, had been a generation apart, not that it had mattered. Mireille had hated him and hated Sarina to the death. He couldn't condemn his wife for *all* her cruelties. He had married Mireille without love, but at his parents' constant urging. To give Mireille her due, she had genuinely tried to make him a good wife. Only a man should never marry a woman he didn't *want*.

He knew which woman he wanted the instant he set eyes on young Sarina Norton, so beautiful she took his breath away. He had never counted on a woman doing that. And Mireille was by no means his first woman. He would carry that vision of Sarina into the next life. If there was one. He wasn't a religious man. What we had was all we got. Let folk have their faith. It didn't do any harm. Then again, he could be in for a big surprise two minutes after lift-off. Some leap of faith there!

A woman's slender form floating towards him in a cloud. An angel, his dark angel. "Sarina?" he called.

"I'm here, Gregory." Sarina moved across the carpeted expanse of the huge room to stand beside his bed. She took his emaciated hand in hers. "Are you sure you can stand the pain?" she asked, looking down at the wraith of the once-invincible Gregory Langdon.

Gregory carried her hand shakily to his mouth. "Tell me, Sarina. Are my grandson and Amelia coming?"

"They are, my dear one." Sarina choked back a sob. "They're due to fly in at noon."

"God, haven't I made a mess of my life?" Gregory groaned. "My son lived in fear of me. News to me, but my grandson accused me of it, anyway. Dev never went in fear of me. Neither did Amelia. Ava was always so quiet and shy. Dev and Amelia were more a pair than Dev and his own sister. Could I have a drop of water, please, Sarina?"

"Of course." Sarina went to the other side of the bed, pouring a little water into a spouted cup. Fears were rising in her. Gregory could well die before Dev and Amelia arrived. She prayed their flight hadn't been delayed. Noel Devereaux had allowed Dev the use of his plane to pick Amelia up. That had been a generous gesture. Gregory and Noel Devereaux had shared a complex past. They had never been friends.

Gregory Langdon was able to swallow a few drops of water. A little dribbled down his cleft chin. Sarina picked up a tissue and very gently dabbed at his chin and dry, cracked lips.

Gregory! Her gaze rested on him. She had thought him immortal. She bent to kiss his sunken cheek. She'd had feelings for Michael, the man she had chosen as her rescuer, but they were as nothing compared to the feelings Gregory Langdon had been able to arouse in her just by *looking.* Many years older, he was nevertheless the man who had taken full possession of her heart. One didn't choose these things. They just happened. She and Gregory weren't the first to be taken victims by fate. Then, as Gregory had begun to age, she had found her eyes resting on another. She had been shocked at that point—how bad could things get? She'd been desperate not to register her feelings, her *lust,* in her eyes. She loved Gregory. But her body had played a bitter trick on her. Her body needed a young man. She had begun to crave Gregory's grandson. Dev, who was bonded to her own daughter.

It had been hell locked up in close proximity to this extraordinary young man forbidden to her. Sometimes she had tortured herself with the notion that Gregory *knew.* She had been really frightened after the monumental row Gregory and Dev had. They were always rowing about something or other, but that time it had to have been really serious. Dev had left.

"Sit with me, Sarina," Gregory was whispering to her, snapping her back to the present. He was clearly in extreme pain.

Sarina drew up a chair. "They'll be here soon," she said in a voice of gentle solace. "I hate to see you suffering, Gregory. You don't want me to call the nurse?"

"No!" The words leapt from his throat, almost as forceful as in the old days. "It's *you* I want, Sarina. You opened up a whole new world for me. Life might have been perfect if we had met at another time, but we got it all wrong. I got too old for you, didn't I, my dark angel?"

She felt a flicker of fear. She was relying on her inheritance to escape. "No, Gregory."

He ignored that untruth. "I sensed it before it happened," he rasped. "But it's all in the past. I was totally out of order when I turned on my grandson. Half off my head with jealousy. That feeling of shame has never gone away. I was jealous, so *jealous,* even of my own grandson."

Fear was unfolding rapidly in her chest. "Don't let's talk about it now, Gregory," Sarina begged.

Gregory took a huge, shallow breath. "No. No point. Stay with me, Sarina."

"You know I will. To the end," Sarina vowed.

The flight to Kooraki took much longer than expected. Take-off had been delayed as a backlog of light aircraft was given clearance. A station hand drove them up to the house. Mel felt so sick and nervous she stumbled up the short flight of stone steps that led to the broad veranda.

Dev took hold of her arm, rubbing it gently. "I'm *here,* Mel." He looked down at her, his expression grave. "We can handle this together."

"What if we're too late, Dev?" She stared up at him, drawing on his strength.

"We did our best. Even my grandfather can't dictate his time of departure from the planet."

They had barely reached the entry to the Great Hall with its bold chequerboard marble floor when Sarina came at a rush towards them. Her olive skin was close to marble-white. Tears were pouring down her cheeks, unnoticed and unchecked. The astonishing thing was that she looked *furious*. "He's gone!" she cried, wringing her hands and making no attempt to embrace her daughter. "Whatever delayed you?" Her voice resounded in the double-storey space, hoarse with grief and open condemnation.

Dev shot Mel a look. "Don't say a word, Mel." His tone was quietly controlled but his eyes blazed. "The world never did revolve around my grandfather, Sarina. For your information, we had to wait in line for take-off. These things happen. You can take us up to his room now. We really don't need your censure."

Sarina sobered visibly. "Forgive me, but Amelia could have come days earlier." She knew she was in no position to take on the splendid, the commanding James Devereaux Landon, who even now made her blood run hot.

"She's here *now*," Dev clipped off. His stomach was churning as he sensed the violent sensations that were running through Sarina.

Sarina turned to lead the way. The reception rooms, living, dining, lay to either side entered through archways. The grand staircase with its beautiful metalwork as delicate as lace curved away to the right. Sunlight fell through the huge stained-glass windows on both storeys. A portrait of a beautiful dark haired, dark eyed woman faced them as they moved up from the first landing. It was a magnificent bravura painting circa eighteen-hundred that bore a resemblance to Sarina.

Maybe that was the reason Gregory Langdon had bought the painting. Dev had often wondered why his grandmother hadn't ordered the painting to be taken down but perhaps she had blinded herself to the likeness.

They were moving down the gallery to Gregory Langdon's suite of rooms when Ava emerged, hurrying towards them, arms outstretched. It couldn't have presented a more striking contrast to the way Sarina had greeted them. Ava wasn't smiling. It wasn't the time to smile, but there was love and warmth in her face. Relief, too, that they had come.

Ava was the real angel in the Langdon midst. A gentle person pitted against a high-octane family. Dev and Ava were alike enough to be twins—the blond hair, black-fringed aquamarine eyes, fine-chiselled features, the Langdon cleft chin, which was more a shallow dent in Ava's case. It was their personalities that couldn't have been more different. Dev had looked after Ava her whole life, and he was deeply upset when she had married Luke Selwyn.

Ava went to her brother first, throwing her arms around him and burying her head against his shoulder before turning to Mel.

"Too long since I've seen you, Mel," she said, tears in her eyes. Both young women went into a heartfelt hug.

"I've missed you, too," Mel said. "I'm so sorry it had to be on this occasion." She couldn't bring herself to say *sad*. Gregory Langdon might have been an incredible man, but he'd had difficulty in expressing his love for just about everyone. Except Sarina. No wonder it had incurred so much jealousy, hatred and despair.

"Who's with Granddad?" Dev asked his sister, putting a hand on her shoulder.

"Dad, of course. A few of the others."

Ava, though beautiful and gifted in so many directions— she painted beautifully, was a fine pianist—was just the daughter of the family, her given role to marry well. This was a man's world. No question. Mel was one female who had rebelled against it, even if she knew running a vast cattle station like Kooraki really was much too tough a job for any one woman.

"I won't go in," Mel said when they were outside Gregory Langdon's door. "I'm not family." Gregory was dead in any case. Her mother's attitude had upset her dreadfully. It was always Gregory Langdon in life and in death. Had Sarina loved her poor father at all?

Well, *had* she?

When had Sarina first fallen under Gregory Langdon's spell or was it vice versa? When had she become his mistress? That was a subject never to be approached. It was wrong, so wrong, the great wall of silence. It had always put a tense and very uncomfortable strain between her and Dev. It couldn't have happened, surely, when her mother and father lived on Maru Downs? It couldn't have happened when Mireille was alive. Mireille would have watched them both like a hawk.

Would they have *dared*?

You bet they would.

Dev didn't insist. He nodded to Mel, signifying her decision was okay with him, before putting his arm around his sister, leading her back into the bedroom. Mel and her mother were left alone.

Speak to me, Mum. I'm here. I'm really here.

Sarina kept her head down, her expression deeply introspective.

"That was a wonderful welcome, Mum." Mel broke the silence, trying to find pity in her heart.

Sarina's glossy dark head shot up. "How could you expect a welcome at a time like this?" She stared back at her daughter with huge black lustrous eyes.

"Oddly enough, I did. Just goes to show how little I

really know you. But then, all I know is what you *wanted* me to know. You turned into Gregory Langdon's creature."

Sarina made a most uncharacteristic move. She lashed out at her daughter, striking her across the face. "How dare you?" she cried. "I never want to hear such a thing again."

Mel didn't deign to touch a hand to her hot smarting cheek, thinking she actually heard her heart break. "I won't say it again, Mum. I've said it once and I meant it. You put both of us into a prison for which Gregory Langdon had the key. I, for one, am not sorry he's dead. He was a tyrant. And you became a hollow woman. Don't forget I'm *my* father's daughter. Someone has to speak for *him*."

Sarina looked genuinely shocked. All thought of Michael Norton, her dead husband, appeared lost to the past. "Why would you hate Gregory so?" She gave Mel a black look. "He did so much for you."

That provoked Mel's fiery response. "Even now you bypass my father for him. Open your eyes, Mum. He did it for *you.* You were his captive. He brought you to Kooraki. You were the real reason he gave Dad a promotion. He wanted you around. The man dominated your life. He tried to dominate mine but that wasn't on."

"Well, he's dead now, Amelia," her mother said starkly, fearing where her daughter might go with her accusations. The thing Sarina admired most in her daughter she also feared. Mel said what she thought. She didn't keep it locked away inside her as *she* had done all her life.

"Then I'd say neither of us will be welcome within these walls. We're *outsiders,* Mum."

Sarina blinked fiercely. "I know Gregory has looked after me."

"Of course! You got it right from the horse's mouth."

"When did you start to become so hard, so unforgiving, Amelia?" Sarina asked in a fierce whisper.

"When I overheard Mireille Langdon calling you a conniving slut," Mel said jaggedly. "Remember how I attacked her. You had to pull me off. I was desperate for us to move out after that."

Sarina's beautiful face worked. *"Where?"* She kept her cry muffled, although the door of Gregory Langdon's bedroom was so thick and heavy it was virtually soundproof. "I was turned out of my parents' home," she cried emotionally. "How could I endure it all over again?"

A loud roaring filled Mel's head. "Finally the truth!" She threw up her hands. "How about that? *Turned out?* The story was you escaped. Mum, was that a total cover-up? I'm even beginning to wonder if every word that comes out of your mouth is a lie. Why were you turned out? For that matter, why did you make your way to North Queensland? Australia is a vast place. You could have shifted to anywhere in Victoria or New South Wales, not travel thousands of miles. You and your secrets! Going to take them to the grave, are you? You've made life so complicated. What to believe, what not to believe. Yet you seem quite comfortable with your inventions. I find it horrible to think my own mother may be a pathological liar. You've never let *me* in. For all I know, you never let Dad in. But I bet you told Gregory Langdon your whole desperately sorry story. In bed. How did you manage it? When did you manage it? Did he have you on Maru when Dad was away on a muster? Did Gregory send him away? I wouldn't be a bit surprised. Gregory was your great anchor in life, wasn't he? Not my dad, Michael."

"No!" Sarina burst out, making Mel recoil at the level of protest.

Her breathing had speeded up so much Mel had difficulty speaking, "No, what?" There was an iciness in the pit of her stomach. It was spreading to her limbs, her arms and her legs. She didn't think she could prevent herself from turning into a pillar of ice. "No, what, Mum?" she repeated in a choked voice. "You're not going to tell me Gregory Langdon was my father?" The cold waves had turned to a roaring tsunami. "I think I'll kill you if you do. Or kill myself."

Sarina was the very picture of outrage. "You're crazy—*crazy!*" she cried, vehemence in her black eyes. She turned away to slump into one of the baronial-style chairs that were lined up at intervals against the wall. "Gregory Langdon was *not* your father, Amelia. I insist you beg my forgiveness. And his. On your bended knees if you have to."

Mel's eyes locked on her mother's. "I'm too busy asking myself if I know you at all. I won't be begging forgiveness, Mum. Anything was possible with the two of you. *I'm* the one who deserved better. I spent my time fighting your battles for you. I was only a kid. Why couldn't you fight your own battles? There are plenty of strong women out there that do. Women left with half a dozen kids to rear alone. You would have received government assistance."

Sarina didn't deign to answer. When she did look up there was stony condemnation on her face. "Don't presume to judge me."

Mel emitted an incredulous laugh. "You're a shape-shifter, aren't you?"

"And what would *that* be?" Sarina asked with scorn, unfamiliar with the term.

"It's a person who can change into anything he or she needs to be to get what they want."

Sarina gave her small secret smile. "Would that you had such a talent. You have no heart, Amelia. There is something bitterly wrong with you."

"Well, it would have to be me, wouldn't it? Not *you,*" Mel countered. She had such an *empty* hollow feeling inside her, not unmixed with dread.

"You show no respect. I can't condone that," Sarina said. "I have just lost the man I revered with all my heart."

Mel tried hard to subdue her anger. She looked long and hard at her beautiful mother. "God help you, Mum," she said, sadly shaking her head. "It seems to me you'll shed a whole lot more tears for Gregory Langdon than you ever did for my dad."

Sarina's full mouth twisted. "I did shed tears for Michael. You think you know about life, Amelia. You know *nothing*."

"And whose fault is that?" Mel asked quietly. "Why did you banish all the photographs? There were no wedding photos. No treasured mementos. The only photographs were of me. Anyone would call that strange. You told me it was your way of dealing with the pain of loss. Why is it I now doubt that? Dad was young. You were both young. God, Mum, you don't look anywhere near your age. Is that a lie, too? If you dressed differently and did your hair more stylishly you could almost be an older sister. What did you do that you had to distance yourself from your family and everything you had ever known? This is the stuff of fiction."

"Life *is* stranger than fiction, Amelia." Sarina jabbed a finger at her daughter as if to underscore her point. "I needed to cut all ties. It's easy enough to disappear if you need to. Outback life is like flying under the radar, anyway."

Mel felt a strong sense of unreality. How could you live with a person most of your life, love that person, then find out you didn't know them at all? Sarina had spun a web of lies around herself. Mel had never seen any wedding certificate. She had seen as a matter of course a copy of her own birth certificate. Michael Norton's name was on it as *Father,* Sarina Cavallaro-Norton, *Mother*. "Cover your face, Mum," she said sadly. "Cover it in shame."

Sarina only looked back at her daughter with her great brooding eyes. "I have no need to atone to you. So say no more. My life is not *your* life. Don't think it is. You have a life of your own."

A sense of hopelessness lay like a heavy burden on Mel's shoulders. "So I'm supposed to accept you're a made-up person?"

"Just leave it there!" Sarina reiterated in a fury. "If you have any love for me at all. I am not a bad woman. I am just a *different* woman."

"You didn't murder anyone, did you?" Mel asked, only half joking. She knew her mother's black moods when the shutters came down.

The heat of fury was in Sarina's flawless cheeks. It was as though Mel had touched on a nerve that was still raw and enormously painful. "How dare you? What I did was fall pregnant. There you have it!" she cried as though she had only confessed under torture. "My parents showed me no support or compassion for such a transgression. I was *adored* all my life, treated like a princess. Then they decided to hate me. My father looked at me with such disgust in his eyes. He turned on me savagely, became a stranger. I should have known he was half in love with me."

"Oh, Mum!" Mel visibly recoiled.

"Don't judge me!" Sarina cried. "His anger wasn't that of a father. It was that of a jilted lover."

For a moment Mel, herself, wanted to disappear in a puff of smoke. "Am I supposed to believe this?"

Sarina gave a mirthless laugh. "I don't care what you believe. I was frightened, but I didn't think it could be so bad. My mother never went against my father. Never spoke up for me or herself. Mireille Langdon, may she burn in hell, wasn't the first one to call me a slut. My own mother did. I will never forgive them for turning against me."

"Mum, you have to tell me more," Mel begged. "I'm not

judging you. Who, then, is my father? Not Michael?" A crushing sadness settled on her heart.

"He was less of a man than I thought," Sarina snorted.

"So you're confirming it wasn't Michael Norton?"

"What does it matter?" Sarina's voice was taut enough to snap. "One thing I know. I suffered terribly, but I never will again. I don't need to be questioned by you. You brought me nothing but trouble."

Mel's heart shrivelled. "That has to be the worst answer any daughter ever heard."

"You expect far too much of me, Amelia," Sarina said. "Suppose we leave it at that? I have no intention of going into details. Some things are best left alone."

CHAPTER FOUR

Mourners came from near and far, by air and over land—family, friends, representatives of the big pastoral families, business partners, lawyers, a heavy sprinkling of VIPs all overdressed for the heat. Everyone, it seemed, wanted to pay their last respects to this extraordinary man who had built up a vast business empire.

Nothing could have kept Sarina away. She stood apart from the chief mourners, but so stunning in a form-fitting black dress, expensive shoes and black hat that no one could fail to spot her without gasping. Her lovely full mouth was compressed, but her black eyes were defiant—some said triumphant—as if to give notice to all and sundry: *I have a perfect right to be here.*

Mel looked on, heavy-hearted. It was as though her mother had a glamorous identical twin who had elected to stand in for her. She had spent many years trying to understand her ultra-reserved mother. Now she realized she hadn't scratched the surface. She too stood well back, experiencing that all-pervading sense of unreality. Sarina had swept the last rug out from under her feet in admitting Michael was not her father.

Who, then?

She meant to find out. She had been fobbed off and lied to long enough.

* * *

It was Ava who kept her company. She and Ava had always had an untroubled relationship. Lovely, graceful Ava was blessed with a soothing manner and a compassionate heart. But Mel, knowing her so well, realized Ava was caught in an unhappy marriage. She had gone into it so rashly. It took living with someone to find the flaws. Mel had uncovered one of Luke Selwyn's predominant flaws right at the beginning.

When Dev had arrived on Kooraki he had taken charge. Erik was beginning to think he no longer knew his place in the world. The dominant figure in his life was gone. He was devastated. There was no way he thought he could step into his father's shoes. At the graveside, he became aware of Elizabeth, his estranged wife's hand slipping into his.

He turned to look down at her, his expression revealing the immense comfort just her touch gave him.

"We'll get through this, Erik. Keep strong."

He couldn't reply for the lump in his throat. Elizabeth had said *we.* Surely he could take from that she still cared for him. Could he be blessed enough to win her back? Did he deserve to? There had only ever been one woman for him and that was Elizabeth. He should never have brought her back to Kooraki. That was the worst of it. He couldn't have gone against his father, who expected him to carry on as usual. In the end Elizabeth had grown to detest his parents. He had thought she had come to the funeral to offer support to their children, Dev and Ava. Now it appeared she was here to offer support to him if he wanted it.

He longed for it with all his heart. All that had stood between them was now gone. He would go down on his knees and beg Elizabeth to come back to him. He would do anything she wanted. He was quite prepared to give up Kooraki, had his father left him in charge. Only he knew his father too well. Gregory Langdon would have left the keys to his kingdom to the man capable of keeping that kingdom not only intact but enlarging it.

He wasn't the man. Just admitting it made him feel a great surge of relief.

"I've missed you so badly, Lisbet," he murmured as, hand in hand, they retreated to the Land Rover to drive back to the house. "It was all my fault." His emotions were so extreme, a big man, he found himself trembling.

"Dear Erik, please don't upset yourself. I was at fault, too. The two of us have been through such a lot, but by the grace of God I feel we've been given a second chance. I've prayed for it."

At that heartfelt disclosure he turned Elizabeth into his arms, holding her as though he would never let her go. "You know I won't hesitate to give up the reins. What *you* want is the only thing important to me."

Elizabeth laughed, even with tears standing in her eyes. "He's probably handed them to Dev, anyway, my dear."

He felt his own mouth twitch in response.

The mansion was crammed with people. Sombre for as long as it took, it had turned into more of a social catch-up. Most were eating and drinking, partaking of the lavish spread, as though expecting a world famine. There was no sign of her mother, Mel saw. Sarina had disappeared. She was no longer Kooraki's housekeeper. She wasn't even the person she had been. Sarina, with the expectation of a legacy, had morphed into someone else, someone independent, free of all the old restraints. Mel cringed inwardly at the thought of what Gregory Langdon had left her mother. She had the certainty it would be a sizeable sum. Above and beyond the usual services rendered. The gossip and the cruel jokes would start up again.

From time to time she felt Dev's eyes on her. They were tracking one another while remaining apart. She felt his strength reaching for her but she held back. She wasn't family. Ava, in a perfect black dress that contrasted with her camellia skin and golden hair drawn back in a French knot, moved from group to group, accepting condolences. A few strands had escaped when she had taken off her wide-brimmed hat. Now they glittered like golden filaments around her lovely fine-boned face. Her husband, Luke, moved with her, charming to all and sundry. It dawned on Mel that Luke was sending far too many glances in her direction. Luke, the womanizer even on his wedding day. He had actually tried to kiss her during the reception. She'd been quick to put the distressing incident down to the number of glasses of champagne he had downed. Her thought then, as now, was that Ava should never have married him. Luke Selwyn wasn't a man of substance. Or integrity. Worse, he had a roving eye.

The house was chock-a-block with flowers, all flown in. Banks of flowers and ornate wreaths had covered the casket. Such a heavy fragrance was in the house Mel found it overpowering. As the crowd had shifted and moved on, she had caught some of the whispers behind hands.

What will she do now? What will happen to her now her protector's gone?

The whispers would never go away. Her mother was just too beautiful and her stunning appearance today was a further eye-opener. It was given to few women to be able to utterly bewitch a man, a man of the calibre of Gregory Langdon. Not only bewitch him but hold him against all the odds. It was easy to fall in love. It was far more difficult to keep that love alive. Nothing would ever be the same again. Nothing would bring Gregory Langdon back. His glorious/inglorious reign, depending on one's point of view, was over.

Across the huge living room, Dev was talking to the O'Hare family. Flame-haired Siobhan O'Hare, the only daughter, was staring up at the strikingly handsome Dev as though there couldn't be a man alive to match him. Mel didn't blame her. Dev had always known and liked Siobhan. She was warm and friendly, eminently eligible as a prospective bride for Dev. The O'Hares were big landowners, with a pioneering history to match the Langdons and the Devereaux. Siobhan was very pretty, very bright, Outback born and reared, educated to university level in Sydney. Siobhan O'Hare was an ideal choice for James Devereaux Langdon. Mel knew just about everyone in the room would agree. Even *she* agreed. Her mother's long "association" with Gregory Langdon had put a taint on their relationship. Much as she loved Dev and battled with her anguished feelings, she wasn't the right match for him. Her dubious background had ensured that. Dev didn't need a wife who brought with her so much tawdry baggage.

Just as she was thinking of making a move upstairs, Dev joined her, after weaving deftly through the crowd. "How's it going?"

"Why do they do it?" Mel asked, deflecting a direct answer. "This is a wake, isn't it? Most of them look like they're at a party. Makes you think."

"It's the drink," Dev said. "Not safe to drink at funerals. Have you any idea where your mother is?"

How strange was that? "Lord, I'd be the last person to ask," she said wryly.

"Maybe she's packing as we speak." Dev gave her a tight smile.

Mel shrugged a shoulder, trying to hide the pain of utter disillusionment. "Could be. Your grandfather has left her provided for."

Dev nodded agreement. "I'm thinking a couple of million."

"And that paid for how many sexual encounters, do you suppose?"

"I would say Sarina put a high price on her own worth.

Anyway, what's a couple of million when you're worth a couple of billion all up?"

"Dear God!" Mel's voice was constricted with strain.

In his formal dark clothes he looked stunningly handsome. The thick waves of his beautiful blond hair caught and held the light. "Maybe I'd better prepare you," he said.

She felt a rush of trepidation. "Prepare me for what?"

"Like I need to tell you? My grandfather cared for you, Mel."

"You mean he cared for Sarina's daughter."

"If you want to think of it that way. My grandfather has looked after Sarina. Fine. I don't have a problem with that. It's my educated guess he has looked after you, as well. Which means you need to sit in on the will reading."

Mel had no option but to appear calm. She was aware people were looking their way, unaware the air around them appeared to others to be charged with electric energy. Most people had greeted Mel in friendly fashion, congratulating her on finding a place with the top-notch merchant bank, Greshams. To others she would always be *That Woman's Daughter.*

"I'm not coming to any will reading, Dev," she said flatly.

He took her arm. "I'll be right there beside you."

"No." She shook her head. "Do you have any idea if my mother will attend? She hasn't confided in me. I don't know who she is any more." For a brief moment she considered telling him what her mother had said. But it was neither the time nor the place.

"Did we *ever* know?" Dev shocked her by saying. "What a difference a death makes! Today, the day of my grandfather's funeral, your mother has chosen to look absolutely stunning."

"She was just masquerading as a housekeeper."

"You mother's lifelong strategy has been pulling the wool over your eyes, Mel. Keeping us all in the dark, for that matter. She's been an excellent housekeeper. No one can deny that. She trained the household staff so well they've been able to handle things today in her absence. With no warning, she simply quit."

"Maybe your father was informed?" Mel hoped that was the case.

"No," Dev confirmed.

Mel stared down at the magnificent antique Ziegler Sultanabad rug, focusing on the beautiful muted colours and the exquisite motifs as though fascinated. "I can't get my head around what's happening here. My mother is actually *two* people. Could it be late-onset schizophrenia?"

Dev stared down at her beautiful face, seeing how very upset she was behind the calm. "It usually strikes *young* people, Mel. I can't imagine a crueller condition, the structure of your brain split virtually overnight. Your mother is as sane as they come. She's exactly who she chooses to be at any given time. I think, with my grandfather gone, she's finally coming out into the open."

Mel exhaled an anguished breath. "What a searing assessment." She was feeling more and more out of place here, among these people with their privileged backgrounds. She should never have come. She should have stuck to her guns. "What will she do now?" she asked bleakly. "It breaks my heart, but she doesn't want *me*. She never wanted me. She told me she fell pregnant by *mistake*." Mel lifted her dark head to stare into Dev's jewelled eyes. "That's me—a mistake."

"Stupid woman!" Dev swore beneath his breath. "She's probably jealous of you, Mel."

"Has it ever struck you, Dev, my mother looks ten years younger than her age? I've always put it down to her beautiful Italian skin."

"*Your* flawless skin." Today, beautifully made-up and

dressed so elegantly, Sarina Norton would have passed for a woman in her late thirties.

"I'm going upstairs now." Determination firmed Mel's classic features. "I can't stay here. When news gets out your grandfather left my mother a lot of money it will only confirm the rumours. It's as well my mother appears set to embark on a new life."

"Now she's free of her chains," Dev said satirically. "But don't *you* think of leaving, Mel. I won't let you."

"Really?" She rounded on him, her dark eyes flashing fire. "And how do you propose to stop me?"

"You'll find out if you try to leave before the will is read. We need to know where we are, Mel."

"I know where *I* am." Mel threw up her lustrous head. "I'm the Outsider. Always was. Always will be. I can only take on what I can handle, Dev. You have to forget me."

His handsome face set into a dark golden mask. "Are you mad?"

"On the contrary, I'm being realistic. It will be all the better for you, Dev. Marry Siobhan O'Hare. You like her. I like her. Everyone likes her. She's actually *ideal*."

Dev gave her a long hard look. "Except, *actually,* I don't feel anything remotely like love for her."

"Love isn't the total package." Mel was afraid she would make a spectacle of herself by bursting into tears. "Think about it, Dev. For all we've shared, I'm not *right* for you. Siobhan *is.* She hasn't taken her eyes off us. Doesn't that tell you something? She and her family have high hopes."

"Then there's disappointing news in store for them," he said with diamond-hard intent. "Siobhan might think she fancies me, but she'll recover as soon as she meets the right guy." He detained Mel by taking her arm. "Please don't run away, Mel. Not yet. My mother wants to talk to you. She thought of herself as an Outsider, as well."

"Your family would have sucked the life out of anybody," Mel retorted. "Of course I'll speak to your mother. She was always kind to us."

"Then let me take you to her. Dad can't let her out of his sight now she's here. He still loves her, you know. He never stopped."

"What price love?" Mel asked in a deeply resigned voice.

Mel tried to shake all her disturbing thoughts out of her head as they approached Elizabeth Langdon. Dev handed her over, then left the two women to a few valuable minutes alone. Elizabeth, a refined, attractive woman, impeccably dressed with lovely chestnut hair and dark amber eyes, looked at Mel with genuine affection. "You're staying on for a while, aren't you, dear?"

"I'm not exactly sure, Mrs Langdon."

"Elizabeth, please," the older woman insisted. "A few days, surely?"

"Probably," Mel answered.

Elizabeth patted her arm supportively. "I'd like to hear all about what you've been doing before I go back. You always were a clever girl, Mel. And the way you used to stand up to my mother-in-law!" She gave a low gurgle. "That was truly memorable. I've never forgotten it. So young and you had more courage than I did."

"Maybe it's because I *was* so young," Mel suggested with an answering smile. "It's so good to see you again, Elizabeth. I wasn't sure if you were coming."

"I'm here to support my children, my darling Ava in particular. Dev has always stood on his own two feet. Now I see my husband needs support. We never did get a divorce," she confided softly.

"I'm certain he's most grateful for your presence," Mel said, knowing it was true.

"What's happened to your mother?" Elizabeth asked with a tiny frown. "I don't see her anywhere."

"I think she's being discreet," Mel managed.

"Difficult when you're such an outstandingly beautiful woman," Elizabeth said rather dryly. "First time I've seen Sarina in years, yet she grows amazingly *younger*." To Elizabeth, Sarina Norton had always been an enigma. Initially she had felt sorry for the widowed Sarina, but she could *never* read her. Never get behind the inscrutable mask. Her little daughter, however, had been blazingly upfront. "She should get well away from here," Elizabeth advised in a serious but kindly voice.

"I'm pretty sure that's her intention," said Mel.

Mel didn't know what her mother's intentions were. Sarina had wanted her here for Gregory Langdon's sake only. She wasn't prepared to talk. Even now she would be bitterly regretting what information had been shocked out of her about her early life. Truly, Sarina had gone through her life like a performer in a play. Michael Norton had committed himself to looking after her and her newborn daughter. Michael Norton had given them both love. Sarina's story wasn't closed. It was wide open as far as Mel was concerned.

She walked the long gallery to her mother's room, desperate for finality. She needed to know who her biological father was. Anyone would accept that, but it simply hadn't occurred to Sarina. She had to be pathologically self-centred, taking little account of the feelings of others.

Outside her mother's door, she rapped hard, feeling the tight pressure in her chest. Things between her and her mother had changed forever. Sarina would have little difficulty cutting ties.

Sarina took so long to come to the door, Mel thought there was no point in hanging around. For all she knew, her mother, away from the intense scrutiny of others, could be crying her heart out. It was all *wrong*. She had only one child, and a smart-thinking child. She had no memory of seeing her mother in tears in the long weeks and months following Michael's tragic death. She had always supposed her mother had hidden her tears, preferring to grieve in private. How wrong could one be?

She was turning away when the door opened. Her mother stood there, still in her expensive black dress, the coldest expression on her beautiful face. It might have been an unwelcome stranger come to her door. This upset Mel immensely. Never in a million years had she anticipated her mother could be like this. She had thought their relationship was loving.

The loving was all on your side.

"What is it, Amelia?" Sarina looked determined to keep it short.

"May I come in, Mum?" Mel heard and didn't like the pleading note in her voice. "I need to talk more with you. You must understand that."

"It does no good." Still Sarina stood back, allowing Mel to enter the large room. It had been redecorated at some expense, Mel saw at once. Her mother had a spacious bedroom with an en suite bathroom and adjoining sitting room. Here, in her private quarters, Sarina had made a bold statement. The décor had a rich, almost opulent, feel with striking colour combinations at great variance with the pastel tones of old. Sarina had used desert colours, burnt orange, sienna, gold, cobalt and a deep coral red. There was a striking painting on the wall, a desert landscape by a famous Outback artist. Gregory Langdon must have given it to her. No way could her mother have afforded it. He must have given her all sorts of things, Mel suddenly realized. But all trace of tears had been wiped from Sarina's matt cheeks.

"May I sit down?" Mel found herself asking of her own mother.

Her mother gave her an odd look. "Of course. You must know I'm extremely upset with you, Amelia."

"I'm sorry about that, but I've given you no good reason to be."

"No *reason,* after the abominable things you said to me?" Sarina reacted as though Mel had committed treason. "You called me—your mother—a *liar.*"

"But you *don't* tell the truth, do you?" Mel countered. "I'm a grown woman holding down a pretty important job, yet you continue to treat me like a child. Everything has been on the 'need-to-know or no-need-to-know' basis. Anyone would think you were in a witness-protection program. It's got to the point where I'm prepared to believe anything. You've hidden yourself away on Kooraki all these long years. What are you afraid of? Or was it simply you loved Gregory Langdon? You couldn't bear to be parted from him. And he, *you.* That was the big scandal of our lives, but an *open* secret. Perhaps you can find it in your heart to tell me your plans for the future? I'm aware they may not include me. If that's the case, why don't you come right out and say it?"

Sarina settled herself into a deep-seated armchair upholstered in an exotic print that appeared to match the *real* Sarina's personality. There was a particular scent in the room, a mix of perfume and some kind of incense.

"How is your relationship with Dev going?" Sarina asked instead, her tone oddly intrusive. "Don't ever expect him to marry you, Amelia. I know he *has* you but he'll never marry you."

Mel was genuinely shocked. Was her mother deliberately setting out to hurt her? What was her strategy? "Excuse me, Mum, but you sound like you'd mind a great deal if he *did.*" She held her mother's dark gaze with her own.

"It won't happen," Sarina stated flatly, as though privy to inside information.

Maybe she was. Maybe Gregory Langdon had given his grandson a shortlist of eligible young women to consider. Megan Kennedy and Siobhan O'Hare were certain to be included on that list.

"We're not talking about me, Mum," Mel pointed out as calmly as she could. "We're talking about you. I can sort out my own life. No way would I ever become anyone's *mistress!*" It was out before she could withdraw it, a retaliatory blow that hung heavily in the air. Perhaps her lack of insight into her mother's unfathomable personality could be attributed to the amount of time she had spent away from her—boarding school at twelve, the years at university, then her job. For the first time in her life Mel felt her mother could abandon her just as easily as she had abandoned her early life.

Sarina's dark eyes glittered coldly. "You can leave, Amelia. This is my room. I'm stuck in it until I leave."

"Perhaps that's because you quit without notice," Mel pointed out.

Sarina stood up, gesturing hard. "I don't want you here in this frame of mind."

"So now I'm an intruder." Mel had to cast off her feelings of being bereft. "Who *are* you, Mum? You're as skilled at concealment as a chameleon. Please believe I wish you every good thing in life. I hope you get all you feel has been denied you. You're a beautiful woman and, as you already seem to know, a *rich* one. If you can ever let go of Gregory Langdon's memory, you may wish to marry again. It doesn't seem like you want to share the rest of your life with *me.* After all, you always chose Gregory Langdon over me, anyway. What I came to find out is—are you attending the will reading?"

Sarina didn't hesitate. It was as though all the humiliations, the torments she had suffered in the past, hidden behind a falsely serene manner, came roaring to the fore. "I'm looking forward to it, Amelia," she said with great satisfaction. "Any link I've had with the Langdons is broken. With Gregory gone, they no longer exist. I'm free at last to be the woman I was meant to be. I'll be moving out of here as soon as possible. I'd advise you to do the same. These people don't want us. I know Dev has always been your fantasy, your superhero, but it will *never* work out. You won't have him. You'd be wise to heed what I say. He might use you, but marriage is out of the question. You will *never* be Mrs James Devereaux Langdon. You will never be his choice for a bride."

It was clear to Mel that her mother was gaining considerable satisfaction from saying this. "You wouldn't *want* him to marry me?" she challenged.

Sarina's great dark eyes flashed. "My poor naïve child, he *won't*."

"Which doesn't stop me from loving him. I'm always going to love Dev."

"Then it's going to be very painful for you to watch him marry someone else." The flare of hostility was unmistakable. "By the way, Gregory provided for you," she added as though Mel didn't deserve it.

Mel stood up. "I don't want any legacy from Gregory Langdon." Her body was braced as though expecting more blows. "I'll give it away. There are plenty of deserving charities."

Sarina's laugh held outright scorn. "Who gives away money? Accept it, Amelia. One can do *nothing* without money. Take it. Then leave this place. There's nothing for you here."

"Nothing for you, either," Mel retorted. "I tried to tell you years ago but you would not be told. I'm smarter than you, Mum. And stronger. I'd rather live a solitary life than subjugate myself to a man's will."

Incredibly, Sarina's black gaze appeared *amused*. "It's been a long time, Amelia, but payback time has arrived. Unlike you, I'm not too proud to take Langdon money. I *earned* it."

"And we all know *how*."

Mel walked in a daze to her own room at the far end of the gallery. Hard to come to terms with the fact that her mother didn't really care about her. Even worse to contemplate, Sarina could well be a pathological liar. There was no concrete evidence to back up her new revelations. If Gregory Langdon wasn't her father any more than Michael was, then who? A man who had abandoned the young woman he had made pregnant? A man to despise.

Mel put up a hand as she became aware there were tears streaking down her cheeks. She hadn't even known she was crying. She never cried. She had always tried to be brave, fighting her own and her mother's battles. Now she had to accept Sarina was two people. .

CHAPTER FIVE

THROUGH the open French windows leading out onto her room's balcony, Mel witnessed the steady exodus of mourners. She took refuge behind the sheer fall of curtains watching Dev accompanying the O'Hares to one of the station vehicles. A small fleet was on hand to transport those who had arrived in their own planes and those who had chartered flights to the station airstrip. The O'Hares' huge sheep and cattle station was some hundred miles to the north-east, more towards the centre of the vast State of Queensland.

She saw Dev shake Patrick O'Hare's hand. Next he bent his handsome blond head to kiss Mrs O'Hare's cheek, before turning to the petite flame-haired Siobhan. It was at that point Mel covered her face with her hands. Her heart crashed inside her. She loved Dev so much. No other woman would love him as much as she did, but she had the terrible feeling her life was about to implode. She would lose him, if she ever really had him. Her mother's taunt came back.

You will never be his choice for a bride.

Gregory Langdon had married a highly eligible woman he had never loved—a marriage of convenience uniting two powerful families. Dev could make the hard decision to do the same. Siobhan was such an attractive, happy and confident young woman, he could well find himself falling in love with her given a little time. A marriage between the Langdons and the O'Hares could bring big benefits to both sides. Siobhan had no big question mark hanging over her. Right throughout history, passion had carried people away. But in the end physical passion wasn't enough to base a life on.

Mel turned away, finding the zip at the back of her black dress. The will would be read in the library, a room exceptionally generous in size, beautifully proportioned, with very fine crown mouldings and twin chandeliers hanging from ornate plaster roses. It was a room that could easily accommodate a crowd, let alone a dozen people. Her mother was to be one of them. She shuddered at the thought. Sarina Norton, Kooraki's housekeeper for close on twelve years, had overnight shed her former persona, transforming herself into a force to be reckoned with.

God knew how much Gregory Langdon had left her. Mel wanted *nothing* from his will herself. Whatever it was he had left her she would donate it. Breast cancer research, premmie babies, a donation to the Royal Flying Doctor Service. She would take steps to do good with Gregory Langdon's money, though she couldn't brush aside the fact that he had been a philanthropist on a grand scale.

It might take a while but when the coast was clear she would head down to the stables and take one of the horses out. Just gallop and gallop and keep going until she came to the edge of the world. She desperately needed to be alone. The knock on her door startled her, she was so lost in her thoughts. Ava, perhaps? They were friends. Her dress half sliding off her, she pulled it back up, adjusting it on her shoulders, before redoing the zip.

Only it wasn't lovely, compassionate Ava standing in the doorway. It was Dev. There was an expression on his face she had never seen before. It was as though he had realized he was going to be handed the reins of power. Even before the will was read he had stepped into the role.

"What is this, Mel?" He crossed the room to her, catching her by the shoulders, staring down at her so intensely he might have being trying to fix her image for all time. "You look very distressed." Her eyes were glittering with unshed tears and her warm golden skin looked unnaturally pale.

"That's because I am." Mel's voice splintered. "I shouldn't have come here, Dev. My mother has entered a new phase of her life that doesn't include me. What do you want? I'm not attending any will reading. I couldn't bear it."

"Who's forcing you, Mel?" There was a decided edge to his voice. Above average height, she had taken off her highheeled shoes. Now he loomed over her, six foot plus, his sculpted body lean and hard. "You've spoken to your mother again."

"I don't want to talk about it, Dev. She's not here, in any case. Her twin stayed on. The twin is going to take the money, then leave. I'm sure you won't see her again."

"It's not going to be as easy as all that." Dev's voice turned hard.

"What do you mean?" She felt another worry. "Is there something else I should know?"

"Your mother won't leave *with* the money," he said crisply. "Settlement could take time. A lot of time, maybe. I don't think we'll be in any rush."

Mel pulled away from him. "You really dislike her, don't you? I suppose you never liked her."

"Why would I?" Dev retorted, eyes brilliant. "She regarded my grandparents' marriage as a mere inconvenience."

"What about *him?*" Mel exploded.

"They both went off the deep end. What do you expect of me, anyway? I have no saintly attributes. I'm a Langdon. My grandmother mightn't have been anyone's idea of a nice gentlewoman, but she had good reason to be jealous of Sarina. Jealousy is a very powerful emotion. People *kill* when caught in its grip. The knowledge her husband preferred a servant over her must have stuck in Mireille's throat. She would have thought she had no option but to try to drive your mother away."

"Only she had no hope of doing it. Your grandfather was all powerful, manipulating us all. My mother and I were *forced* on your grandmother."

"Indeed, you were," Dev confirmed bluntly. "Sarina would never have been able to escape my grandfather's grasp if he wanted her."

She could feel the tide of anger sweeping up in her. "History isn't going to repeat itself, Dev." Her lustrous dark eyes flashed.

"Oh, cut the melodrama, Mel." Dev was all hard impatience. "In many ways you've put me through hell. It's the humiliated *child* in you taking a stand, the *I'm not going to be my mother* thing. You're *nothing* like your mother, Mel. You're an entirely different person. You have fire and pride, beauty and intelligence in combination. Only you have to see *who* you are before it's too late."

The message, delivered in a deeply frustrated and deadly serious voice, resounded in her ears. "So there it is—the ultimatum. I've been expecting it. Why have we never been unable to let each other go, Dev?"

"It's perfectly simple," he said acidly. "I must be out of my tiny mind!" When he spoke again, his tone was modified. "I know what you've had to go through, Mel. God knows I've been patient and I'm not a patient man. When did I fall in love with you? Maybe when you were seven and I was nine? Even then I wanted to protect you."

"So you had two little sisters, Ava and me?" Her voice was woefully off-key.

The blaze in his eyes gave fair warning. "Don't go there, Mel," he said in a deadly quiet voice. "My grandfather might have desired Sarina from the moment he set eyes on her but you can't damn a man for his desires. You can't damn him for wanting some happiness in life. Who are you to judge him? Well? Go on. Answer the question," he challenged with a good lick of censure.

Mel sat down, her nerves horrendously on edge. "It's easy to conjure up darkness from a heavy veil of secrecy, Dev. I know *you* had your doubts at one time."

A ray of sunlight fell across the room, dipping his blond head in gold. "To harbour passing doubts isn't unnatural, Mel," he said testily. "To hold onto them *is*. I want you to come downstairs. I want you to sit with me while the will is read. I know it will be painful, but I don't want you to hide away up here. My grandfather gave many things to you, most importantly your education. You've never had to struggle. You didn't have to haul yourself up the ladder. You were supported. You owe my grandfather, even if you try to shut that fact away. You've always shown courage, even fearlessness. Do it now."

"Under orders?" She threw up her dark head to stare at him, so superbly, arrogantly *male*.

"A request, Mel," he said.

Mel didn't answer. She rose, a graceful figure, her hands going to her long, thick hair. She had pulled the pins out of her aching head. Now she needed to rearrange her hair in a coil.

"Leave it," Dev said. Her beauty, her endless allure and her vulnerability was breaking over him, ripples spreading out strongly from his centre, threatening the control he needed to maintain. By some miracle, things might come right. Mel had struggled so long to reconcile all her conflicts, her heartbreaks. The situation with his grandfather and Sarina had dragged them all down, Mel more than anyone. But she had to understand he had reached his limit. There was no place for indecision left in his life.

Showdown time, Mel thought.

Feelings in the library were running dangerously high. Mel received quiet acknowledgements. Nods here and there. None of them appeared as distant as she had anticipated. Maybe the clan had a more benign view of her than they had of her mother. Despite her entrenched defences, she found herself relieved.

When the revelation came that Sarina Norton, Kooraki's former housekeeper, had been bequeathed twenty million dollars it came like a massive king hit. For long moments one could have heard a pin drop in the huge book-lined room, such was the seismic shock. Even the expression on Dev's handsome face was grim. Two million dollars had been his estimate and Mel had the idea he'd thought that way too high. Mel felt her own prickle of horror and disbelief. Twenty million dollars! So that confirmed it. Gregory Langdon and Sarina Norton, young enough to be his daughter, had been lovers. There was no longer any room for doubt. The cover-up was exposed.

"Dear God!" A muffled exclamation broke from one, seconded by another, then another.

Mel's limbs were locked in tension and a kind of shame. Her mother, at the far end of the second row of chairs, looked neither left nor right. She sat with aristocratic grace amid the wealthy Langdon clan, who sat as though petrified. Mel had taken her place well to the back. She had agreed to come. Sometimes she thought she would do anything for Dev. But she had refused to sit beside him. Not even within touching distance. Dev, who could pick up on all her signals, knew better than to try to persuade her otherwise.

Another bombshell, but nowhere approaching the same magnitude. She, Amelia Gabriela Norton, had been left two million dollars. Far more money than she could ever have saved in her life. No way was she jumping for joy. She hadn't asked for it. She didn't want it. Her charities would. To no one's surprise, James Devereaux Langdon had been handed the reins of power. In truth, they all had secretly nominated him the right man for the job.

Erik Langdon, one of the few genuinely grieving Gregory Langdon's death, far from letting fly with multiple resentments, as some of the clan might have expected, looked unperturbed by his late father's decision. He sat calmly with his estranged wife, although that no longer appeared to be the case as they were holding hands. Erik Langdon had inherited more than enough to last him a dozen lifetimes. He didn't have to bear the burden of heading up Langdon Enterprises, even with all the people they had working for them, the accountants, the bookkeepers, the high-priced lawyers, the various boards and their members. It was not a life he had been suited for. On the other hand, it had been easy to tell from an early age that Dev had been cut out for the job. Hadn't Gregory been grooming him for years until that final roaring, raging split about which both men had kept silent?

In many ways Gregory Langdon and his grandson were alike, Erik thought, tightening his grasp on his wife's elegant long fingered hand. They were the movers and shakers. Not him, though he couldn't think he was all that incompetent. He wasn't. Only he hadn't come up to his father's exalted standards. He was one of the lesser mortals. It didn't matter now. His parents were gone. He had other plans. Plans for himself and his long-suffering wife. No other woman he had met compared with Elizabeth. He didn't blame her for shifting far away from Kooraki. His mother, Mireille, had been a spectacular troublemaker, the worst in their feuding families, the Langdons and the Devereaux, with a particularly cruel tongue. He almost had it in his heart to understand the path his father had taken. It was like they said. If you couldn't find love at home you'd find it elsewhere. His father had been a very sexual man. A man of strong passions. And he had wanted Sarina Norton, that strange unknowable woman.

Did Sarina, who he had spent years addressing as Mrs Norton, feel guilt or shame at the wrong she had done her young daughter? Erik wondered. Amelia had been a highly intelligent child with a real understanding of what was going on around her. Beautiful, enigmatic Sarina Norton had been a huge embarrassment to them all and worst of all to her child. Amelia had suffered real damage. No child should ever be under constant attack. It was Sarina Norton's fault. She could have left. She would have received help. His mother would have paid her anything to go away. But she had elected to stay. Now they all knew why.

Erik and Elizabeth heard with pleasure their lovely Ava, who had married so unwisely, was now one of the richest young women in the country. Would that affect her marriage? Elizabeth wondered. The marriage wasn't a great success, though Ava never complained nor spoke ill of her husband. The handsome husband, Luke, was pleasant enough, although totally eclipsed by Dev. The Selwyns were well-to-do people, quite the socialites. It seemed no amount of money could buy Ava the happiness she craved and she had deserved much better in life. Erik felt both he and Elizabeth had failed one another and ultimately their children. On his part, it was a lack of strength, the courage, the backbone, to take a stand against his father's overwhelming presence. Time now to measure up.

Erik Langdon turned to his wife. "Everything okay, dear?" He could see clearly that she was upset.

Her head hovered close to his broad shoulder. "May

Gregory rest in peace," she said very quietly. "But I can't think a one of us wants him back."

"Not even Sarina," Erik whispered.

"She always put Gregory above her own daughter," Elizabeth murmured sadly. "Do you suppose she feels guilty about that?"

Erik didn't hesitate. He answered with an emphatic, "No!"

Luke Selwyn waited for the opportunity to catch up with the beautiful Amelia. She was a gorgeous creature, so glamorous with exotic looks, full-lipped mouth, come-to-bed eyes and a slow sexy smile. She was the polar opposite of his angelic, near-breakable Ava. He still carried the titillating memory of the little tussle he'd had with Amelia at his wedding reception, just holding her sleek body in his arms. For some reason, even given the time and the place, he had been desperate to kiss her, if only for a moment. He knew about her and James Langdon. Even he could feel the sparks around them but he was certain Langdon would never marry her. She was the housekeeper's daughter—a housekeeper, now an extremely rich woman. History had its courtesans. They were a species who would always survive and prosper. But beautiful Amelia had no real status in the clan's eyes. He knew a great many young women were seriously attracted to Langdon. When he married, he would marry well. Maybe the O'Hare girl.

"Wait up a moment, Amelia," he called, moving quickly to the foot of the curving staircase. He was determined to have a moment alone with her, though he knew he had to be careful. Langdon could just knock his block off. Langdon, the king of the castle! Amelia seemed to be a bit of a craze with him. Her story ran parallel to her mother's. Luke had often fantasized about Amelia. She was *hot* when his Ava was cool to the point of frigid. Who knew, Amelia might be able to slot him in somewhere? Langdon was on Kooraki. She worked in

Sydney with Greshams. Greshams was very hard to get into. She had to be smart. A smart girl could juggle any number of men.

Mel tried hard to control her irritation. Why on earth was Luke running after her? He would only be stirring up trouble. She knew he found her attractive. It actually made her feel sick the way he made a beeline for her whenever they happened to meet up at functions, dinner parties or the odd occasion when he invited himself to lunch with Ava and her. Her instincts told her he was fully prepared to betray Ava with a little something on the side. Maybe he had brainwashed himself into thinking she might be agreeable. Men of all ages thought no woman they were interested in could turn them down.

Keep it low-key. A few civil words, then be on your way.

His tone was low, openly admiring. "You look wonderful!" Luke mounted two of the steps.

"You look well, too, Luke," she responded coolly. "Is there something you wanted to see me about?"

"Well, I rarely get to see you." He smiled. "I'd love to catch up. That's all." While he spoke, his green and gold-flecked eyes were moving over her in a way she really disliked. "Maybe you could come back downstairs so we can talk."

"I think not," Mel said, roused by the sound of voices inside the library. "You and I haven't much to talk about, Luke." She kept a watchful eye over his head for either Dev or Ava, though she knew both had been deep in conversation with their parents when she had left the room.

"Sure we do," he responded with a bright smile. He had excellent white teeth, cosmetically enhanced. "Why don't you visit us more often?" he asked. "Ava and I really value your friendship."

"Ava and I like to catch up without you," Amelia said briskly. "Ava's not a fool, Luke. Far from it. She knows about your roving eye."

He appeared flustered. "You never told her?"

"What do you take me for?" Mel retorted, her voice sharp with contempt. "There's no use your pursuing me, Luke. We both know what this is all about. You fancy me."

"God, yes!" he groaned. "We could be careful." He snaked out a hand to take her wrist, his thumb savouring the satin texture of her skin.

She peeled his hand away, feeling repulsed. The urge to slap his smug face was so irresistible, she had a job controlling herself.

"Your father has the reputation around town for being a womanizer. Following in his footsteps, are we?" she asked, raising supercilious brows.

Luke only laughed. His good-looking face assumed a knowing expression. "Name me any top businessman in the city who doesn't have his bit on the side. It's the way of the world, Amelia. You know that. Doesn't your precious Dev have his affairs? It was really hotting up there with Megan Kennedy. I was told that for a fact. Only something went wrong. I figure he's going for the little redhead these days. What's her name, Siobhan O'Hare? Or don't you know what's going on, my beautiful dear thing? You're on the market, aren't you? There aren't going to be any miracles for you, Amelia. My wife and I do discuss family matters, or did you think we didn't? I know you and Dev have had a thing going for years, but it's never *simple,* is it? In the family's eyes, you and little Siobhan aren't in the same class."

Mel couldn't control her emotional reaction. "Goodbye, Luke," she said with tight control.

"Ah, Amelia, now you're cross with me. I didn't have to

spell it out, did I? You know the score." He kept following her up the stairs.

Mel swirled round. "Get lost, Luke. You disgust me."

"I can live with it," Luke persisted, lost in an agony of lust. His gaze slipped down over her. He loved the way her black dress curved around her body like the petals of a tulip. Her breasts were so beautiful. Any man's eyes would linger on their shape and fullness. He could feel himself hardening, pent up and excited. "Can I help it if I want you?"

"Any woman is for sale?" Mel was on the point of pushing him back down the stairs.

He gave a throaty chuckle, sickeningly, amazingly confident. "You're not as indifferent to me as you like to make out, Amelia. Don't go silent on me. We go back a long way." He caught her arm.

"Personally, I prefer to forget that," she said sharply, unaware she was grinding her teeth.

"Yeah, well—" Luke's face contorted. "We didn't get far, did we? I was drunk—"

He got no further as a man's voice sliced through the air with all the menace of a hurled knife.

"Let her go, Selwyn."

Luke flushed alarmingly. He was instantly aware of his precarious position. He released his grip on Mel, exaggerating his jump back from her, only to lose his balance. He wobbled dangerously before bracing an arm on the balustrade. Even then he landed with a stagger on a lower step of the stairs.

"That was super, Luke!" Mel said with contempt. "Do it again."

Only it was no time for levity. Dev was walking towards them, an electrifying figure, six foot three of hard muscle with the physical strength Luke Selwyn couldn't hope to match. The expression on his face said *furious.*

With difficulty, Luke Selwyn swivelled to face his brother-in-law, hastily arranging his handsome features into what he hoped was a reassuring smile. "Slow down, man. I was just having a few words with Amelia. Don't get to see her often."

"So what were you saying she didn't like?" Dev snapped back, blue-green eyes slitted, his voice so hard Luke felt desperate to be on his way.

"Nothing really, Dev."

Mel, too, experienced a wave of alarm. Dev's expression was so formidable anything could happen. He moved nearer Luke, his right fist clenched. Mel gave a stifled gasp. "Everything's okay, Dev." She was aware of the flush of blood beneath his dark golden skin. She couldn't believe this was happening. Dev looked perilously close to knocking his brother-in-law to the floor.

Luke must have felt the same because he was focusing all his attention on getting away. "Sorry if you got the wrong idea, Dev."

"You would be the one to be sorry," Dev ground out.

It was appallingly clear to Mel that Dev didn't seem to be looking for an alternative to beating his brother-in-law up. The only one who could probably put a stop to this was Ava, Mel thought. She rushed down the stairs. She had to calm the situation. Then, like a miracle, Ava appeared, regarding the fixed tableau with anxious, even appalled eyes.

For a long moment there was an aching *stillness*, then Ava spoke. "Whatever is the matter?" She stared at each one in turn, the expression on her lovely face strained.

Luke took the heaven-sent opportunity to rush to his wife's side, while Mel offered a halfway plausible explanation, keeping her tone light. "Luke came a mite too close to taking a tumble down the stairs."

"Gave me a bit of a fright," Luke blurted, looking the very picture of white-faced innocence. "That's never happened to me before."

Was Ava going to swallow it? Mel asked herself, holding her breath. Ava was no one's fool.

"Always a first time," Ava retorted, sounding all of a sudden extremely brisk. "Okay, then. I'm going up to our room. Come with me, Luke. Your face *has* gone pale."

"Shock," he said with more a rictus than a smile on his handsome face. "It's a wonder I didn't twist my ankle."

"That would have been rough," Dev cut in suavely. "Better watch it next time."

Ava shot a swift searching look at her brother, then she took her husband's arm, steering him towards the staircase. "Can we meet up in an hour, Mel?" she asked over her shoulder.

"Sure. Come to my room. We can have coffee on the balcony."

"I'll be there," Ava confirmed.

Dev waited until his sister and her husband had disappeared before asking the inevitable question. "What was that all about?" His brows were drawn together.

Mel tried for flippancy. "Beats the hell out of me!"

"That guy is unbelievable," Dev said grimly.

"That he is. I thought for a moment there you were going to challenge him to a sword fight."

Dev wasn't in the mood for jokes. "He always did fancy you," he said, rocketing back into anger.

"Please!" Mel shuddered.

"I know all the signs," Dev continued. "Lust."

Mel tried to keep calm. "I won't take that personally."

He looked at her, making a big effort to calm his feelings. "You're a powerfully sensual woman, Mel. You create excitement."

"Thanks a lot. So it's *my* fault?" Her volatile temper sparked.

"Of course." This time he answered smoothly, with a hint

of humour. He lifted her face to his, planting a staggeringly erotic kiss on her mouth.

"Dev, I'm thinking someone might come." Startled, her senses swirling, she drew back.

"*I* thought about it. So?" His jewellike eyes glittered. It came to Mel, not for the first time, one needed great eyes to be truly charismatic.

"So there's enough talk as it is." She lifted a finger to her pulsing mouth. She didn't think she could exist without Dev's kisses but she wasn't about to tell him that. She had to keep her passions well below the surface. Become adept at it like her mother. "I'm trying to be as unobtrusive as possible."

He laughed briefly. "You don't do unobtrusive, Mel."

"I don't flaunt myself, either," she shot back.

"Selwyn thinks you do." His voice held a faint taunt. "It's like a damned soap opera around here."

"And it's not a joke, Dev."

"Who said anything about a joke?"

"You're forever winding me up."

He gave her the smile that was her undoing. "God knows that's easy enough. You don't just jump to conclusions, Mel. You take quantum leaps."

Who knew better than he? "I think I'm functioning reasonably well, thank you."

"You're functioning *extremely* well, but you do admit you have problems, Mel. Consequently, *we* have problems. Life for us has been one seething cauldron of emotion."

"Families *are* the great cauldron for brewing up trouble," she reminded him. "Especially your family."

Dev's handsome face darkened. "Don't forget Sarina." He had a mad impulse to say more but held himself in tight check. Sarina Norton, that strange woman, had always had her own agenda. "You couldn't beat Granddad for delivering seismic shocks. He looked after Sarina *exceedingly* well.

Apparently, the going wages of sin these days is twenty million dollars. But hey, it's good to progress in life," he tacked on satirically.

"You don't beat about the bush, do you?"

"Do I ever?"

The air around them had heated up. Nothing new. "Rumour has now become *fact*. It's abundantly clear to us all my mother looked after your grandfather pretty well."

"Looking after a man will do it every time," Dev offered very dryly.

"Is that what you want from the woman in your life, Dev?" She stared up at him.

"I always thought *you* were the woman in my life," he answered, as cool as you pleased. "Are you or aren't you?"

She looked away. "Maybe I've got to be a habit."

"Absolutely fine with me," Dev responded in his maddening fashion. "I have to say your mother is a piece of work. She didn't even officially quit. She just downed tools."

Mel couldn't suppress a moan. "I don't know what to say to that except I'm sorry. But really, what did you expect? You don't often meet a housekeeper who knows in advance she'll have millions in the piggy bank. There's a lesson in it for us all. It pays to keep your mouth shut. Now I'm continuing upstairs, Dev. We're well on the way to having one of our monumental blues. I'd say in the next few seconds."

"A blue works for me." Dev took a gentle but firm hold of her arm. "However, I appeal to you not to start one. Especially with a house full of people. You're not the only one to find this whole situation both embarrassing and humiliating. Then today of all days, with Ava only a short distance away in the library, the lecher Selwyn decides to chat you up."

Mel relaxed slightly. "He's the sort who likes to chat women up," she said. "Luke thinks he's a real stud. It's the high-end ego thing. Mercifully, you don't have it."

"Excuse me!" Dev looked affronted.

Mel could only manage a wry laugh. For all he had going for him, Dev had absolutely no narcissistic leanings. "Put it down to the fact he'd had a few drinks," she said. "There's no need for concern."

"But there *is!*" Dev insisted. "Let's go outside."

"Why?" She made a show of resistance, just for the hell of it.

"I *said* so. Look, Mel, in a minute or so they'll come streaming out of the library. I don't want to be here." He began to steer her away. "Selwyn knows what will happen if he bothers you again, but it's Ava I'm worried about. The sooner Ava gets rid of him the better. There's time. She's young. She can start again."

"I'm sure *he* doesn't want that," Mel said, believing it to be true.

"He doesn't love her," Dev muttered grimly.

Mel sighed. "I don't know if he's capable of it. But I do know he's peacock proud of her. Ava is very beautiful—"

"And she's very *rich,*" Dev added with a blaze of temper. "She wants to talk to you. You have a chance to find out if being married to Selwyn is what she really wants. If she wants out, then she simply has to say so. He won't be getting his hands on her money. Grandfather insisted on an iron-clad pre-nuptial agreement. I don't want to see my beautiful sister locked into an unhappy marriage. I've seen first-hand what unhappy marriages can do. At least there isn't a child to worry about. There's been quite enough unhappiness," he stated bluntly.

"Another good reason to hate the rich," she only half joked.

"Granddad's solicitor is the only one not in shock," he said wryly.

"I imagine he's used to shocks. It must happen a lot when

wills are read. I'm so glad your grandfather looked after Ava. A woman needs her own money."

Dev gave a short laugh. "I agree. You stand on your own two feet, Mel. Ava has always admired you for that. She envies your achievements."

Mel shook her head. "I haven't set the world on fire. I'm no brain surgeon. By the way, I don't intend keeping the money your grandfather left me."

"Disgusted, are you, with your lot?"

Mel ignored the taunt. "I'm going to give it to organizations that really need it. I have charities I support."

Dev frowned. "But it's not much, surely, Mel? Think about it," he said seriously. "You can always make donations as you see fit."

"And I see fit to give away the lot. Why is it the truly rich don't seem to know they're rich?'

"I suppose they don't know any different. Dad didn't seem perturbed Granddad handed over the reins to me."

"I guess *he* saw it coming. We both know your father looked on the top job as an intolerable burden. Now he can live the life he wants. Your mother wants to come back to him. He certainly wants her."

"So at least one good thing has come out of all this."

They had moved out of the Garden Room, filled with a cornucopia of luxuriant plants and golden canes in huge planters, into a private walled garden. The heady swirl of fragrances acted as stimuli for the senses. Butterflies and dragonflies in a kaleidoscope of colours hovered over the abundance of blooms, near drowning in the nectar. The sky, even at late afternoon, was still a glorious dense blue, trailing silky white ribbons of cirrus cloud. Above them a great wedge-tailed eagle patrolled his domain. The sun beat down hot. A magnificent electric-pink bougainvillea streamed gracefully over the top of the trellis and through its walls, golden sunlight shafting through it here and there. Dev broke off a papery pink flower and pushed it into the gleaming dark coil at Mel's nape. "The amount of time we've wasted," he mused with deep regret.

"I don't blame you if you're tired of it all, Dev. The conflicts have affected me far more than you. You came from a position of strength. I didn't. We've both admitted we had a passing fear we could be related by blood."

"Do you think I don't know how much that's preyed on your mind?" Dev said. "Gregory, for all his sins, was *not* your father. None of us believed it. Not even my grandmother, no matter what she implied. One thing alone, the timing was way too tight. Are we to believe his passion for Sarina was so overwhelming he took her, a newly married young woman, virtually on sight?"

"There have been such cases," she said with a dismal laugh. "You mustn't forget how many dreadful encounters I had with Mireille. My mother seemed impervious to the endless humiliations Mireille heaped on her. I wasn't. And I was only a child."

"A child who possessed a high degree of fearlessness and integrity. If you really want to lay every last fear to rest we can always undergo DNA testing. Just say the word."

"And thereby slay the dragon."

"It would deal with your last vestige of doubt."

"I don't have any," she said, shaking her head.

"Neither do I."

"It was just one of my neuroses."

"My grandmother had a lot to answer for," he said grimly. "She tried to poison your mind."

"In my formative years, too."

Deep, deep in her subconscious, a memory abruptly surfaced. A memory she had safely buried. Now it returned.

Mireille Langdon was dead, but she could see her very plainly. Familiar fear and anger bloomed in her chest.

"You stay right where you are, you insolent little girl," Mireille thundered, her handsome face livid, working with rage. *"How dare you speak to me in that fashion?"*

She was frightened but she wasn't going to back down. "How dare you say terrible things about my mother?" Mel cried, straining just to breathe.

"Your mother!" Mireille threw back her dark head and laughed. "That conniving slut. Her face and her body might be beautiful but her soul is black. One of these days she's going to push me too far, mark my words, child. I could get rid of Norton, the poor cuckold, who sprang out of nowhere and was given promotion. Without him, you and your mother would have to pack up and go. I can guarantee it. Let it be known Mireille Langdon is mistress here. Your mother is a servant. No, don't you dare come at me with arms flailing, little girl," Mireille warned. "I admire you in a way," she said with a terrible despairing sigh. *"You've all the guts your immoral mother hasn't," she snarled, her spirit in the merciless grip of the malevolent green-eyed monster. "My husband isn't the only one with power, you will see. I am a Devereaux. I don't stand alone."*

Dev's voice jolted her back into the present. She couldn't credit now the way she had physically attacked Mireille Langdon when she was only a child. But someone had to defend her mother. She had taken on the role of champion. Not needed it would now appear. Sarina had struck her own powerful bargain.

"You're coming down to dinner?" Dev was asking.

"With the clan?"

"Not a one of them classier than you, Mel."

"But I'm the enemy, aren't I? Or the daughter of the enemy. Pretty much the same thing. The millions Mum got, they could have shared. They represent millions lost."

Dev rested both hands on her shoulders. "I'm not losing any sleep over it, Mel. My advice to you is get over it. Change your therapist."

"Therapist?" she scoffed. "I don't have one. I don't actually know anybody who does."

"Talking to the right person, someone with experience and wisdom, could help get things out of your system." It was said with more than a hint of seriousness. "Maybe a few sessions?"

"You think a *few* would cure me?"

"Maybe we never say goodbye to the child within us," he mused, keeping his arm around her and walking on.

"Why would we? Childhood affects every last one of us. Good memories. Bad memories. Love or rejection. The stand families take can result in bitterness and estrangements right down the years. Relationships founder because they're not deemed *right*. I know in your family's eyes I'm not right for you. Even *I* don't think I'm right for you. The media could get hold of my mother's story. That involves me." She was aware of the widening implications.

"Well, twenty mill was right out of the ballpark, Mel," he said caustically.

"You're the CEO now, Dev. Would you consider contesting the will?"

"And wash our dirty linen in public?"

"I take that as a no, then, shall I?"

His arm tightened. "Mel, the last thing I want is to hurt *you*. That was worded badly but you know what I mean. Your mother can take the money and disappear for all I care. She had a right to a slice of the pie, but not a fortune."

"The biggest reward your grandfather could offer." Mel sighed. "It all makes me feel very sick. And sad."

"Don't think it doesn't sadden me, too. But everything is a nine-day wonder, Mel. Bigger stories sweep in to take priority. Did your mother drop the slightest hint when she'd be leaving? It's not as though she can call a cab."

"She's not the woman to confide," Mel said, feeling utterly betrayed. "She's advised me to leave. She didn't say with *her*."

"She's not, alas, a contender for Mother of the Year," Dev returned dryly. "She should be aware she's not dealing with Dad any more. She's dealing with *me*."

Mel's expression was accepting of that. "She doesn't need any prompting from me to see that. I'm sure she'll beg a word."

"Terrific! I can't wait."

They had almost reached the very romantic-looking white latticework pavilion at the end of the arcade. Mogul in appearance, it had been one of their favourite trysting places in the old days. To be alone in the witching hours. To make love.

I'm with you. With you. And my blood is singing.

Dev always said the most beautiful things. She had often told him he should have been a poet. She had no doubt of his love.

Then.

"Come to dinner, Mel. I think we can be certain your mother won't be joining us."

"I can't think she was expecting an invitation." Mel's tone matched his for dryness. "She'll know everyone is furious about her mind-blowing legacy."

"Like she can't handle it?" Dev asked with scorn. "Your Madonna-faced mother is in reality one tough cookie. I'd been thinking set limits, Mel, but that got blasted away. But

I suppose, when it comes down to it, it was my grandfather's money. It was his wish she have it."

Mel gave way to her entrenched bitterness. "Why, if he loved her, didn't he marry her when your grandmother died? It was such a reason for shame. My shame, *her* shame. My mother hung in there."

"Maybe she knew the big payout was coming?" Dev's tone was as dry as ash. "We have to face it, Mel. Your mother always had her own agenda. Being a loyal and loving daughter, you've been in denial. There wasn't going to be the fairytale ending. My grandfather thought it best not to marry her." As he spoke, he was acutely aware of the rigidity in Mel's body, the warring feelings that continued to hold her in their grip.

"She fitted better as a mistress. He was Gregory Langdon, cattle king. She was Kooraki's housekeeper. As Jane Austen would have put it, beneath his station. My mother has a few secrets she thought worth keeping."

"Maybe they're so secret she has a hard time remembering them," Dev shot back.

She wasn't ready to confide in him yet. It was a touch hard when she had no real conviction her mother had been telling the truth. She stared off to the pavilion. How many times had she and Dev declared their undying love? That was when their mouths weren't stopped by passionate kisses. The pavilion, to this day, was covered with a beautiful old-fashioned coppery-pink rambler with strongly fragrant blooms. She thought she would carry that particular scent to her grave.

"Hard for anyone to lay low when they've just come into twenty million dollars. The press *will* find out, sooner or later."

"None of this will touch you, I promise," Dev said.

"Even you can't guarantee that, Dev."

"I'll certainly try. But discovery, disclosure is in the nature of things. Even royalty can't evade it. Our job is to rise above it. Get on with things. Be glad of what we've got."

"Marcus Aurelius, Roman Emperor, said pretty much the same thing almost two thousand years ago. To paraphrase: get out of bed, take up your duty, appreciate what is around you."

"Which only goes to prove great minds think alike," Dev said, his tone smooth as silk. "I want you to join us tonight, Mel."

"So all things must happen in accordance with your will?"

Slowly he turned her to look at him. "Sure you're not a man-hater, Mel?"

"Sometimes." She stared into his beautiful iridescent eyes. "It *is* a war between the sexes."

His smile was sharp. "Well, I, for one, long for it to be over." He fanned the fingers of his right hand across her throat. "Especially when you feel you have to win."

"Only sometimes," she breathed, mesmerized by the man.

"You're winning now." He bent his head, kissing her long and hard for the pleasure and the pain of it. Lingeringly, he ran his mouth over the satiny column of her neck, his hands moving inevitably to the full contours of her breasts.

She stayed him, her hands over his, her eyes brilliantly alive with emotion. "Was it sex that bonded my mother to Gregory? Is it sex that bonds you to me?"

He let her go so abruptly she staggered, flinging out a steadying hand to the trelliswork, stark frustration etched on his face.

"I'll forget you said that. It's high time you felt a whole lot better about yourself, Mel. Until then, talk is futile."

CHAPTER SIX

BY the time Ava joined her, Mel had managed to compose herself. Dev hadn't come after her. He might well have come to the end of his tether. Who would blame him? It was she who had kept their tempestuous relationship in check. Life had set her down in a maze so intricate it required a heroic effort to find a way to break out. Yet few people were able to resolve every issue. She thought she'd been close to a turning point, only her mother's mind-blowing legacy had put paid to that. Her mother mightn't care that she could be exposed to public scrutiny, but *Mel* cared a great deal. Few people knew her background. Now there was the distinct possibility they all would.

She longed for a father. A strong man who would have stood by her. A father she could turn to. Her stomach was tied in knots. She wouldn't have a moment's peace until she found out who had worn that crown. That Michael Norton wasn't her father could be a complete lie. Had Michael truly understood the woman he had married? No answer to that. He had gone and left her and the world behind.

Now she was battling to cope with an additional burden, the memory so recently dredged up. Was it possible Michael's death was somehow Mireille's doing? The thought didn't altogether shock her. Mireille had indeed wielded power and Koorakai was an enclosed kingdom.

* * *

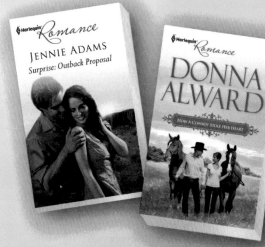

GET 2 BOOKS

We'd like to send you two *Harlequin® Romance*
novels absolutely free. Accepting them puts you under
no obligation to purchase any more books.

HOW TO GET YOUR
2 FREE BOOKS AND 2 FREE GIFTS

1. Return the reply card today, and we'll send you two
   Harlequin Romance novels, absolutely free! We'll even
   pay the postage!

2. Accepting free books places you under no obligation
   to buy anything, ever. Whatever you decide, the free
   books and gifts are yours to keep, free!

3. We hope that after receiving your free books you'll
   want to remain a subscriber, but the choice is yours–
   to continue or cancel, any time at all!

EXTRA BONUS

**You'll also get two free mystery gifts!
(worth about $10)**

FREE!

Return this card today to get
2 FREE BOOKS and 2 FREE GIFTS!

Harlequin *Romance*

YES! Please send me 2 FREE *Harlequin® Romance* novels, and 2 FREE mystery gifts as well. I understand I am under no obligation to purchase anything, as explained on the back of this insert.

❏ I prefer the regular-print edition
116/316 HDL FMPU

❏ I prefer the larger-print edition
186/386 HDL FMPU

Please Print

FIRST NAME	LAST NAME

ADDRESS

APT.#	CITY

STATE/PROV.	ZIP/POSTAL CODE

Visit us at:
www.ReaderService.com

When Ava arrived, looking grave, they moved out onto the balcony. Mel had ordered coffee for two. It had been sent up on a beautifully set silver tray. Her mother had got some things right training the staff. It occurred to her, as it had so often in the past, her mother must have had a gracious upbringing. There was the way she looked, the way she spoke, the things she *knew,* as if she had been accustomed to a fairly privileged lifestyle herself. A huge family rift over a shock pregnancy fitted a familiar scenario. Her mother, too young, had fallen pregnant to an unsuitable man outside the sanctity of marriage? Her strict Italian father, who until that point had adored his beautiful daughter, then banished her as the daughter who had dishonoured her family?

When and where had Sarina and Michael met? She couldn't erase Mireille's comtemptuous *cuckold* from her mind. At the time she didn't even know what a cuckold was. She'd had to look it up. All the questions she could have asked Michael had gone with him to the grave. She had learned she was a 'premmie baby.' Mireille had informed her of that as though it was some kind of a stigma. Another thing Sarina had kept to herself. Again, at that time she hadn't properly understood what 'premmie' meant. For some reason Mireille had always spoken to her as though she were well on the way to being a woman instead of a child.

Ava took a chair opposite Mel, a small circular wrought-iron table between them. "What a day! Something wrong?" She took a closer look at her friend.

Mel looked away across the garden, with the rising fragrance of flowers almost an unbearable pleasure. The great tree canopies over the years had formed natural archways, preserving the shade for massed plantings of the giant-leafed dark green alocasias with their distinctive ebony stems. She turned back to Ava, who was twisting her wedding ring around and around on her finger. "Nothing out of the way. Had a few words with Dev. Neither of us can help it. We always get into our arguments. Some of them can be pretty fiery."

"So sparks fly around you?" Ava spoke as though that was something to be greatly desired. "They always did. But you're soulmates, Mel. What was it about? Can you tell me?"

Mel laughed without humour. "My mother, need I say? I know everyone was shocked today. Myself included."

Ava didn't rush to answer. "We'll get over it, Mel," she said finally. "You take everything so hard. You've taken on your mother's problems all your life. Problems a lot bigger than yourself. You are *not* your mother."

"Only the sins of the mothers can and do fall on the children, Ava."

"Okay, but you're mad to carry any sense of shame, Mel. It had nothing to do with you." Ava had often thought Mel had put something of a brake on her mother's plans. "Give it a little time, Mel," she advised. "It will all blow over."

"That's what Dev says." Mel shrugged. "Anyway, enough about me. What about you? You're not happy, are you?" Mel asked the searching question as she placed Ava's cup of coffee in front of her.

"Thank you." Ava gave vent to a heartfelt sigh. "I thought I'd be finding freedom in my marriage, Mel, but it hasn't turned out that way. I was the trophy wife, a Langdon. Luke is a greedy person. He's immensely self-centred. And he has the potential to be unfaithful, if he hasn't been already. I know he was trying to chat you up," she added with a pained grimace. "I'm not a fool. I'm so sorry about that. Luke thinks he's God's gift to women, just like his father, who has the old 'many a good tune is played on an old fiddle' type of mentality. Luke wants to keep me in a gilded cage. Like a canary, I have to sing his song. I don't have an ally in his parents. As far as they're concerned, he's *perfect,* the handsome dutiful son. If he's got a bit of a roving eye, so what? All men have. It's expected of them. Luke loves me in his way, only his kind of love is suffocating."

"I can see that." Mel took a sip of the rich, fragrant coffee.

"I'm expected now to fall pregnant. Over two years married. High time to hear the patter of tiny feet."

"Only something is holding you back. You don't see Luke as the father?"

"God help me, no," Ava confessed, bowing her shining head as if she felt guilt. "I can speak to you, Mel. You understand. There has been no divorce in our family. Even Mum and Dad didn't file for divorce."

"Because they continued to care so much about each other."

"Yes, isn't that lovely?" Ava's lovely face brightened. "Dad doesn't care about the will. He and Mum have big plans. They intend to travel."

"I wish them all the happiness in the world," Mel said with perfect sincerity. "As for you, we have a new order now, Ava. Dev is not your grandfather."

"Thank God for that!" Ava gave a shaky laugh. "Dev only wants my happiness. I should have listened to him. There were many questions I should have asked, yet I charged full steam ahead."

"Smart women can make bad choices, Ava."

Ava nodded agreement. "I feel like Luke is snuffing the life out of me. But it's all my own fault. I should have listened. I was such a fool."

"We're all fools from time to time," Mel brooded. "We can see where we went wrong with the benefit of hindsight. Sometimes circumstance gives us no choice. Or we don't know in advance how things are going to turn out."

"You're being too kind to me, Mel." Ava lifted her beautifully modelled head. Like Mel, she had arranged her hair in a shining updated chignon. "The writing was already on the wall. You were my bridesmaid. You saw it. A romantic dream in tatters."

"So what's the plan?" Mel, being Mel, took the direct approach.

Ava moaned. "It's going to cause a furore, but I intend to file for a divorce as soon as I get home. Mireille, were she alive, would be furious with me. 'You made your bed, now lie in it.' Can't you just hear her saying it?"

"*She* surely had to and it nearly destroyed her," Mel retorted, unable to forgive Mireille Langdon for the treatment she had meted out to an innocent child. Her mother, however, had been far from innocent.

"Have any of us recovered?" Ava asked.

Mel remained silent. *She* certainly hadn't.

"You're coming down to dinner, aren't you, Mel?" Ava picked up a cupcake, simply for something to do. She didn't want it.

"You must know how your family feels, Ava."

"And you the feisty one! You who used to tell my grandmother off when you were knee high to a grasshopper? You're not a gutless person, Mel. Please come."

Dinner in the formal dining room passed without incident. She was acknowledged with courtesy by everyone, aware she was receiving lots of covert stares when they thought she wasn't looking. She was drawn into the general conversation, though it was obvious to her that her mother's shock inheritance, most improper, loomed large in everyone's mind. The subject wasn't touched on. She knew Dev would not have tolerated it.

It had taken a lot for her to get dressed and come down to join them. She had brought a choice of two suitable dresses, both silk, one a lovely shade of violet, the other black patterned in silver. She settled on the violet, fixing her hair, half up, half down, then hooking sapphire and diamond earrings into her pierced ears. The earrings had been very expensive; her reward to herself for pulling off a lauded business coup.

As a mark of respect to Gregory Langdon, neither Erik nor Dev took his magnificent carver chair at the head of the long gleaming mahogany table that could seat forty when extra leaves were added. The chandeliers weren't turned on, but still the table was a blaze of candlelight. Three tall silver candelabra were set at intervals. Someone had placed a too tall silver vase of exquisite pink liliums as a centrepiece. Its height and the spread of the lovely flowers acted more or less as a screening device. She could see the people she wanted to see anyway.

She watched Dev talking, giving a half smile at times, charming to everyone but with a pronounced gravitas. His blond hair gleamed pure gold in the candlelight, as did Ava's. Both were seated opposite her. During their long talk, Ava had confided many painful personal things. It was obvious she had run out of the necessary mental and emotional strength. The marriage wasn't working. She was more of a symbol than a wife.

"Luke has been intent on controlling me from day one."

Luke was always playing to the grandstand, Mel thought. Ava said it had got to the stage when she could hardly tell the difference between what she had left behind and what she had signed on for. There was a great irony in that. Mel was grateful Luke hadn't come down to dinner, claiming he felt too distressed to eat. What a lie! More likely he found his brother-in-law just too intimidating.

Standing well back in the shadows at the far end of the room, Mel could see a few of her mother's well-trained staff, ready to spring to attention at a moment's notice. After the excellent three-course dinner, followed by coffee—Mel had noticed both she and Ava had hardly eaten anything—members of the family began to excuse themselves, one after the other. A charter flight had been organised for eight o'clock the following morning. It would take them all to Sydney. An early night was in order, as well as providing a legitimate excuse to escape an uncomfortable situation.

In the end Mel was left alone with the new Master of Kooraki. "Thanks for joining us, Mel."

"Don't thank me. I did it for Ava."

"Is there no end to your goodness?" He sat studying her. Her dress was beautiful, with its deep V-neckline showing just the right amount of cleavage. He had never seen her in that particular shade before. It set off the satiny warmth of her flawless olive skin. "Love the earrings," he said. "A little trifle from your mentor?"

She could feel her face flush. "Don't be ridiculous. I bought them myself."

"A beautiful woman should never have to buy her own jewellery."

"You mean when she's having an affair?"

"*Your* words now, Mel," he said with shimmering eyes. They really were a wondrous colour. "I think it's about time I paid a call to your mother," he shocked her by saying.

"What, *now?*" Mel's face was a study in alarm.

Dev took an exaggerated glance at his watch. "It's only nine-thirty. We have the rest of the night. Why don't you pop up and check she's dressed? A little discretion is called for. She might have to change out of her negligee. I bet she's got a few."

"Something wrong with that?" she reacted angrily. She had spent her life defending her mother.

"God, no! Many the time you've lured me onto the rocks

with your gorgeous night apparel," he said, his expression sardonic.

"Not that I got to keep it on long."

His face settled into an expression of patience. "Are you going or not, Mel? Either way, I'm speaking to your mother tonight. She's not calling the shots."

"Easy to see who your grandfather was," Mel responded in a flash. "You're not going to turn into him *right now,* are you?"

"If that's what it takes, Mel," he told her very crisply, indeed.

"Futile to argue. Give me ten minutes."

"*Five,* then I'm coming up."

She almost ran the length of the gallery. No gentle tap on the door. This wasn't the time for her mother to barricade herself in.

Sarina finally appeared, wearing an exotic silk kaftan, the material patterned in brilliantly coloured tropical flowers. "I hope you don't intend making a habit of pounding on my door, Amelia. What's the matter now?"

Mel's response was sharper than any she had given her mother. "Good thing you're dressed. Dev wants a word with you. He'll be up in five minutes."

"*Wha-a-t?*"

Sarina appeared to buckle at the knees. Mel took hold of her mother's slender arm, unconsciously massaging it. "Look, Mum, it's okay. But you can't get away with the Greta Garbo act. Dev wants to know your plans. You can't just hide. You've already insulted the family by quitting your job."

Sarina didn't bat an eyelid. "I have nothing to apologize to the Langdons for," she said loftily.

"I think you do. Wouldn't you call it a breach of contract or something, giving up without notice?"

Sarina's beautiful face hardened. "That's my business, not yours. I want you to go, Amelia. I don't want you here when Dev comes."

"Well, I want to be here, Mum." Mel was prepared to stand firm. "I might be the only person in the entire world on your side."

Sarina looked back at her in such a way Mel felt a chill in her blood. Who *was* this woman? It was obvious her early life had scarred her. No time to think about that now. Sarina was wearing her long lustrous hair loose so it rippled down her back. She was still made up. Her exotic kaftan only complemented what was of late her slightly *wild* beauty. Whatever age she was, her beauty hadn't dimmed.

"Go, Amelia," Sarina said. "I don't need you." She stared back at Mel, who was too stricken to hide her distress. "Go on now."

"It might be best, Mel." Dev spoke from the open doorway. His jewelled gaze was fixed not on Mel but Sarina, who coloured up fiercely.

Mel nodded to him. "Yes," she said dolefully. "I'm only in the way." As she shifted her gaze from Dev back to her mother, she was surprised by the most extraordinary expression on her mother's face. That expression struck Mel mute. Sarina was staring at Dev with absolute *fascination*. She had seen that exact expression on women's faces when they looked at Dev. The one thing in the world she had not allowed for was seeing it on her mother. Sarina, who was still young and beautiful. As a further madness, had she fallen for Dev? Was Sarina the reason Dev and his grandfather had fallen out so violently?

The idea was *revolting*. Had Gregory, who had occupied Sarina's attentions for well over a decade, grown too old and sick? Had Dev then filled Sarina's hungry eyes?

It was *wicked*.

"Mel, what's the matter?" Dev asked her sharply. The look on Mel's face bespoke shock and something more. Disgust. As though some boundary had been crossed that should never have been.

Mel drew back, fearing the possibility she could be making another one of her quantum leaps.

I mean it can't be real. It's indecent.

"Mel?" Dev's gaze was searching.

"I'm staying," Mel abruptly announced.

Sarina took her place in an armchair, habitual calm back in place. "You're not wanted, Amelia."

"I never have been," Mel retorted.

"Stay if you want to, Mel." It was the voice of the man in command.

"Might as well come along for the ride," she returned in an ironic voice. How could she ever begin to fly when her wings were continually cruelly clipped?

The meeting was over. It was brief. Sarina would fly back with the others in the morning. She had graciously consented to give Dev the name of the hotel where she would be staying until she was ready to launch herself on an unsuspecting world. "The world is now your mother's oyster," Dev observed dryly, not bothering to mask his contempt.

Mel said nothing.

"I suppose most people would think that when handed twenty million dollars. Your mother is leaving Kooraki forever. Don't worry about her, Mel. Sarina knows how to look after herself. I wouldn't be surprised if it's not too long before she captures an adoring husband. Think of all the bewitching years with my grandfather."

"Sure she hasn't bewitched you?" It burst from her with violence. It was a wonder she didn't shout at the top of her voice.

"Now, that's disgusting!" Dev caught her arm, pinning her gaze. "You ought to be ashamed of yourself. What the hell are you on about now?"

"Evil!" Mel spoke with loathing, her voice cracking with emotion. "Pure evil. What was the cause of the big break with your grandfather? It drove you away from Kooraki to live with your great uncle. What was it, Dev? It had to be something very serious."

Dev looked with fury, his jewelled eyes blazing. "It's too ridiculous to even talk about. Let's get away from here. We could be overheard." He took hold of her arm, propelling her along the gallery.

Ava must have heard their raised voices because she emerged from her old room, still fully dressed. "Is something wrong? You both look upset." Easy to sense the rift between them. Both were breathing irregularly.

"It's the time for upset, isn't it, Ava?" Dev retorted. "We're all upset. We let people torture us. I say put an end to it."

"Hear, hear! *I* intend to," Ava spoke forcefully.

"Atta girl!" Dev saluted his sister. "Get some sleep. You know I'm always here for you, Ava."

"You're the best brother in the world," she maintained. "Problem with Sarina?" she asked, watching Mel's face. Sarina had been obliged to spend her time bailed up in her room. She had forfeited her position for good and all.

Dev answered for her. "Exhausting as it is to admit it, yes. But Mel and I are going to sort it out."

"Right, Mel?" Ava asked, her beautiful eyes never once leaving her friend's face.

Mel managed a smile. "You're a good friend to me, Ava. You always have been. Dev and I are used to our fiery little chats. You know that. Everything's okay. I'll see you in the morning."

Ava was unconvinced. She could see the sparks flying off

them both like static, but what could she do? "Then I'll leave you to it. Love you both." She blew a kiss.

"Love you, Ava."

Dev and Mel spoke as one while all the while their biggest concerns were elsewhere.

As they neared the staircase, Mel said with fiery determination, "I'm going to bed, Dev. I don't want to talk."

He actually manhandled her, pressing her back against the wall. It was futile to struggle. "You started this, Mel. Histrionics won't save you. What's on your mind? Have the decency to spit it out."

Mel clenched her fists, feeling all of a sudden very sick. "I need to know why you left Kooraki. Was it because of my mother? Did you covet her, too?"

Dev's hands fell away. "Believe that, you'll believe anything." Disgust threw an iron mask over his arresting features.

"So tell me what it was about," she begged. "It has never been mentioned."

"I can't talk about it, Mel, I'm afraid," he said shortly. "I'm just too mad. Mad that *you,* of all people, could ask me such a *revolting* question. Your mother is *trash!*"

No one, not even Dev, was going to get away with that. Even if it were true. She hit him then, using all her strength and she was very fit.

He caught her hand in midair, his eyes ablaze. "Go to bed, Mel," he ordered in a voice harsh enough to make her blanch. "If I were the brute you seem to believe I am, I'd give you a backhander that would knock you off your feet. How's that?"

"Oh, God, forgive me. I'm sorry." There seemed to be a mist before her eyes as Mel fell back on childhood prayers, ironically taught to her by her mother.

"No, Mel, *I'm* sorry," Dev said, perversely kissing her punishingly hard on the mouth. "Sorry for the years I've spent loving you." He turned his back on her, making without a backward glance for the stairs.

Inside her room, Mel collapsed onto the day bed, burying her face in her hands. She had been so much at the mercy of her mother. Nevertheless, it had cut her to the heart to hear Dev call Sarina *trash*. What had provoked it? Dev had never used strong language about her mother. Sadly, she wasn't in any position to dispute the charge. Her mother was getting away with murder, as the saying went. A good thing she was leaving in the morning.

It's your last opportunity to have it out. She won't be expecting a return visit. You'll have the element of surprise. Don't let her just walk away.

Dev had most probably locked himself in his study, disgusted with her. Everyone else had gone to bed. It was a comfort to know all the doors of the homestead were made out of solid, sound-muffling mahogany.

She was surprised to find her mother's door unlocked. Maybe Sarina was expecting a nocturnal visitor, she thought with cynicism. Sarina did have a dangerous allure, and God knew she had used it. She turned the knob. There was silence in the room, but she could hear the shower running strongly.

Mel moved over to an armchair, ready for confrontation.

Sarina entered the bedroom with a white towel wound around her head.

"Peekaboo!" said Mel, totally without humour.

"My God!" Sarina actually jumped when she saw her daughter, sitting for all the world like a judge in session. "You startled me," she said, roused to anger.

"Who would care?" All love for her mother seemed to have dissolved.

Sarina shrugged. "So what's up *now*, Amelia? Think I'm going to tell you more with Dev not around? It's not going to happen. I want to go to bed. You're always on about something. You've been like this since you were a child."

"What a burden I must have been to you, Mum," Mel said. "I'm surprised you didn't have your pregnancy terminated."

"Too late!" Sarina declared cruelly, throwing off the hand towel.

"Shame on you. Shame, shame, shame. You're one hell of a sick woman, Sarina."

Sarina pointed the finger of scorn at her daughter. "More of a woman than you, my dear."

"But I've got Dev," Mel taunted. "*You* haven't. Got the hots for him, Mum? Isn't that a bit pathetic, not to say vaguely incestuous? Did Gregory get too old to perform like the mighty stallion he once was?"

Sarina didn't appear at all fazed. "At his best he would never rival Dev."

"Oh, stop it." Mel gave a contemptuous laugh. "Even now you're trying on another of your big-time lies."

Sarina ruffled a careless hand through her lustrous long hair. "You're getting to be very boring, Amelia. Dev thinks so, too."

Mel was amazed that such calm had descended on her. "How does a human being get all bent out of shape? Dev is in no way attracted to you, Mum. He despises you."

Sarina's great eyes flashed. "As if I'm crazy enough to believe you! You're full of your own malice."

"No, Mum." Mel shook her head. "But you're crazy enough to believe anything."

Sarina drew close to her daughter, speaking vehemently. "At least I've never slept with my own flesh and blood."

Condemnation burst from Mel's throat. She leapt to her feet. "That's the stake through the heart, is it? You'd stop at nothing to separate Dev and me. Are you going to change tack now and tell me Gregory Langdon was my father?"

"To hell with you!" Sarina threw up her hands, nostrils flaring in rage. "Michael Norton certainly wasn't," she barked.

It wasn't possible to be more wounded than she was. "Only who would believe you? You chop and change as you please. It's even possible you don't *know* who my father was! You could be delusional, you know that?"

"I have an ugly past." Sarina spat her fury.

"You must have. Something turned you into a compulsive liar."

"It has been suggested before." Bizarrely, Sarina laughed.

"Dear Gregory, I suppose. Maybe poor deceived Michael? Well, here's the deal, Sarina. Look into my eyes and tell me the truth for once in your miserable scheming life."

"Deal, what deal? What have you to deal with?" A faraway look came into Sarina's great eyes. "My story is my own."

"And that's the best you can do?"

Sarina rounded on her, prepared to lash out. "You're wasting your time, Amelia. Anyway, it's better for you not to know."

"Only I can't go along with that. Neither would anyone with a right to know. Gregory Langdon wasn't my father. A devil in hell prompted you to say that. Dev and I don't need any DNA testing to confirm it. You're eaten up with jealousy and it shows. You can't bear to think Dev might marry me when Gregory wouldn't marry you. That's it, isn't it? Shock tactics. Jealousy and envy has you all fired up, ready to say anything to break us up."

Sarina stood with one hand on her hip. Her black hair was drying and tumbling all around her face. She looked beautiful and half crazy. "You'll break up without me, my girl. I know that only too well."

Mel studied her mother's face and slender body. "How old are you, Mum?" she asked. "You have to be much younger than you've always claimed. How old were you when you had me? Sixteen, seventeen? Savage old Mireille was kind enough to inform me I was a premature baby delivered by a nurse from the Royal Flying Doctor Service. All the years of ugly rumours masquerading as fact were indeed fact. Mireille called Michael a cuckold. I didn't even know what it meant. Mireille could have had Michael destroyed. Ever think of that? She hated you so much she was prepared to do anything to see us off Kooraki, who knows, with Michael in a wheelchair. Or worse, dead."

"You go too far." Sarina gave her a foul look. "But then you have your own demons. Michael's death was an accident. Gregory would have seen to it that we didn't leave. Gregory wanted me from the first moment he laid eyes on me."

"I suppose that has to be true," Mel said dully. "You were pregnant then, a young girl, a first baby, not showing. I suppose you put it over poor Michael. You'd have found it easy manipulating men. Even the great Gregory Langdon. Michael loved me. He believed I was his child. You're such a liar, I probably am."

"Well, you won't know now," Sarina said sweetly. "There are many mysteries in life, Amelia. Best to accept it. Only you're the sort of woman who likes banging her head against a brick wall. There's no way I'm going to explain myself to you. My cup overfloweth with money—lots of money." She laughed.

Mel looked at her mother with great forbearance. "Haven't you forgotten Dev could hold up your inheritance? He's the executor of Gregory's will. Then there's the press."

"Press?" Sarina's eyes widened as her hand flew to her throat.

"Good Lord, Mum, they're going to be very interested in you. A genuine rags to riches story. If you won't speak about your past, the media will drag it up. They're not short on investigative journalists, you know."

For the first time Sarina appeared flustered, then she rallied. "Who would care? I'll be out of the country."

"That's if Dev releases the money."

Sarina put her hands over her ears as though she didn't want to hear a word more. "I did my best, Amelia. I kept you. You should be eternally grateful. I won't have you digging into my past. I won't allow it. It's water under the bridge. Accept it. Dev won't marry you any more than Gregory would marry me. But a man has to have his sexual needs fulfilled. That's where we came in. Dev has always had, shall I say, a soft spot for me. I'll be able to talk him into releasing my money early. Now, go, Amelia. You've always been awkward to have around, with your never-ending questions."

Mel rose to her feet. "They *will* be answered," she said, certainty written all over her. "Take it on board, mother dear. You haven't seen the last of us, Dev and me."

CHAPTER SEVEN

THE birds woke Mel around 5:00 a.m., a dawn symphony struck up from the highest branches in the wild bush. It was played with wondrous abandon by a multitude of voices in all registers. The strings reigned supreme, followed by the flutes, then the reeds, bolstered here and there by contrasting bass voices. It was inspirational to the ear and psychologically effective. Lying there listening, Mel felt better balanced to get on with her life.

Her sleep had been riven with nightmares. The ghosts of the past—Mireille, the wicked witch had figured largely; Sarina with all her dark harmonies fully revealed. Sarina had not only fooled her daughter, she had fooled everyone. Maybe even Gregory Langdon. Although, on her own admission, someone had called Sarina a liar. But it was all over now. Mel felt there was little hope of reconciliation. Sarina hadn't been cut out for motherhood. Not all women were. Even robbed of Dev, the man she loved, she would still want the truth. It was instinctive in every human being who discovered they knew little or nothing about their early life, or indeed about their true parentage. Sadness and disillusionment weren't easy to bear. They were binding chains that had to be broken.

She threw on her riding gear, then made her way through the silent house, taking a back entrance to the stables complex. A good gallop in the crisp morning air would clear her head and settle her nerves. She didn't expect the lads to be about yet, but she could saddle up her own horse. The finest horses were stabled at night and turned out by day. Ordinary horses were only brought inside in the depths of cold. It was unnatural, in any case, to keep a horse in a confined space for any length of time.

Unexpectedly, as she crossed the courtyard, she could hear voices coming from the tack room—male voices, one very loud, hectoring, full of wrath, jabbering in a tribal dialect. Two younger voices were trying to get a word in. Clearly there was an argument in progress. Did life ever run smooth? She had no intention of turning about. Perhaps she could settle it?

She strode into the room where dozens of bridles hung from their racks, the reins looped through the nosebands, saddles aplenty with all the accessories. The room smelt of all the usual things—horses, hay, leather, liniments. And something else, something *rank.*

The two part Aboriginal stable lads turned to her, clearly frightened, not to say terrified by a menacing presence.

"Good morning." She gave them a quick encouraging nod before turning to the ancient man, who stood his ground. He looked scary enough to spook anybody.

She knew him. It was years since she had last laid eyes on him. It was Tjungurra, the sorcerer, who was widely believed to have caused deaths. Tjungurra, the *kurdaitcha* man, whose role it had been to punish all transgressors. He was naked except for a pair of torn and dirty shorts, his emaciated chest hideously disfigured by deep ugly scars that had tribal significance. Bunches of dried leaves were tied to his arms. On his snow-white head, the hair wildly tangled, he wore a filthy scarlet headscarf. Brilliantly coloured parrot feathers hung from his long beard. In the old days no one would have dared cross Tjungurra. Tribal people continued to believe in sorcery and Tjungurra had undoubtedly been a *kurdaitcha* man.

The lads, from their fearful expressions, clearly thought he was still operative. Even more alarming, the rheumy black eyes fixed on Mel appeared to hold *hatred*.

"What are you doing here, Tjungurra?" she asked in a crisp but unthreatening voice. She faced the old horror front on, aware the lads were casting uneasy looks in her direction.

For answer, Tjungurra lifted his bony arm, balled a hand into a fist, then shook it at her, jabbering away in his native dialect. He appeared filled with rage. She could only pick up on one word in the torrent that spewed from his lips. She looked back at the old man, startled.

"I'm Amelia," she said. *"Amelia,"* she stressed, pointing to herself. "Sarina is my mother. Are you talking about my mother?"

"Leave 'im be, Miz Mel," one of the lads was brave enough to warn her, even if his voice emerged as a croak.

Tjungurra turned on him and the lad actually shrieked. Even Mel's nerve endings were trembling. "Speak English," she ordered. "What is it you want?"

The old man dared to move closer, causing an escalation in tension.

Why is he here? Is this really happening?

"Sarina," he jabbered hoarsely. *"Saa...ree...naa..."* He drew out the syllables like a length of rope.

It was a lovely name on most people's lips, but there was no music in the way the old man spoke it. It sounded more like a curse.

There was a hard twisting inside of Mel. "How did my father die?" She couldn't control it. She started to shout at the old man. "Tell me or I'll have you locked up. Locked away in a jail. You'd die there, caged like a wild animal. The old woman isn't alive to protect you. She can't take care of you."

The old man threw her a poisonous look, apparently just starting to warm up. He yanked a single brilliant parrot feather out of his beard.

"You don't frighten me, old man." One of the lads had surreptitiously put a whip into her hand. Now she brought it out, cracked it, causing the sorcerer to fall back, though he continued to point the feather at her as though he were a spear thrower.

No one had heard Dev come to the door. They all jumped at the sound of his voice. His tall, powerfully lean figure was silhouetted against the backdrop of brilliant morning light.

Mel spoke impetuously. "Look who's here, Dev. The wicked old man who killed my father."

"Mel!" he remonstrated, knowing how volatile she was.

"He did. He *did*," she shouted, with no way of knowing if it were true. There was a sharp pain in her right temple as though one of her rare migraines was about to start.

Dev reached her in a few strides, getting a firm grip on her arm. "I'm here, Mel. Get control." There was such toughness and authority about him even a sorcerer would think twice about messing with such a man. Moreover, a Langdon. The nomadic Tjungurra had crisscrossed Kooraki all his life.

It appeared Mel's accusations hadn't frightened the old sorcerer. Grinning evilly, he began to move about in a mockery of a dance, though it was soon apparent the movement caused him severe pain in the back and hips.

Dev's order to stop was more effective than Mel's crack of the whip. Instantly the old sorcerer broke off his weird ritual. Dev advanced on him, towering over him, speaking in Tjungurra's own dialect.

"Make him tell you, Dev," Mel implored, filled with an enormous conviction that Mireille Langdon had sought the help of the *kurdaitcha* man. She had it now. Mireille had wanted Michael Norton badly injured or dead. Had she cared? A jealous wife, a faithless husband, the woman who had stolen the faithless man's spirit. Michael Norton had been determined to be the most vulnerable. The easiest and most accessible to become the victim.

Dev looked over the old man's white head into Mel's eyes. "There's no way to make him speak, Mel. He'd die before he'd ever do that."

"Time for him to die!" Mel cried. "What's he doing here, anyway? Has he come for Sarina? Your grandfather is dead. He's heard about it, of course. The old drum system. That's why he's turned up. Is it revenge time? He mentioned her. I'm sure he thought I was her. He's probably gaga, the old murderer."

"I'll have him shifted away," Dev promised her.

"Where is far enough?" Mel cried. "The South Pole?"

With a gesture of his hand, Dev had the lads leave. They moved off in record time. They didn't want to deal with any of it. Least of all the *kurdaitcha* man.

"Someone spooked the cattle that day, Dev," Mel said, believing in her deepest heart that it had been this menacing old full-blooded Aboriginal.

Dev shook his head. "There was no evidence of that."

"*Was?* You know about this?" Her voice rose towards the rafters.

"For God's sake, Mel. It was over twenty years ago. I was a kid like you."

"*Never* like me! You're a Langdon. Even a *kurdaitcha* man would hesitate to kill a Langdon outright. Mike Norton, sure. We know the old monster used to make poison powder. I wonder why Mireille didn't get him to make up a batch for the house."

Dev's dynamic face went taut with strain. "Leave it there, Mel."

"I won't!" she defied him. "Were there sanctions imposed on this dreadful old creature? He would have feared Gregory like everyone else. Gregory wouldn't have had a problem having him killed or worse, locked up for life." Her whole body was shivering although it was hot. "Look at the old devil. He's aligning himself with you."

"He has to," Dev said briefly, his voice tight with control. "His power has long waned. He has no magic against me or mine. Go back to the house, Mel. We'll talk together later on. The plane leaves at eight o'clock sharp. We're rid of your mother once and for all."

Mel pointed to the old sorcerer as if she were pointing the bone. "He killed him. He caused him to be killed. Poor Michael, the innocent victim." She broke down, starting to sob. "You knew all this, Dev," she accused him. "You've known or had your suspicions for years about this bloodthirsty old man. But you had to protect the Langdon name. You people who think you're unaccountable, living like feudal lords in your own private kingdom. The likes of me can go to hell."

"Mel!" Dev implored, summoning up every scrap of his huge reserve of self-control. "We'll talk about this when you calm down." He would think of something to defuse the emotion.

"To hell with you!" Mel was on a roll. She rushed to the door, but not before she saw the old sorcerer nodding vigorously, a hideous grin of glee on his face.

Back at the homestead, she realized there was nothing else for it. Sarina, as *persona non grata,* was more or less confined to her room. Every step Mel took, she felt more and more drawn into Sarina's horrible sticky web.

"Knock, knock, who's there!" Sarina stood in the open doorway, coiled like a spring ready to snap.

"I'm getting awfully bored with this, Amelia. I'm not telling you anything more. I thought I made that clear."

"Don't Amelia me!" Mel pushed her mother back into the room. "Dressed for the trip, are we? Versace silk shirt, beautifully cut designer pants. How elegant you look! You could be any beautiful woman who has known nothing but a life of wealth and privilege. Except you're a total fraud."

Sarina made a derisive sound. "I have to be downstairs in twenty minutes, Amelia." Clearly she thought her daughter a pushover.

"Tough! Let 'em wait! Sit down, mother dear. You don't feel uncomfortable, travelling with the enemy?"

"I sit at the back. I am blind to them."

"You're blind to everything," Mel said. "I'd been intent on a morning ride to clear my head, only I met up with a guy looking for you."

"Me?" Sarina looked startled.

"You'll remember him, I'm sure."

Sarina dropped into a chair, winding her arms around herself. "Who is it?"

"You surprise me, even now. *Is* there someone looking for you?"

"Amelia, there's no time," Sarina protested sharply.

"Take a guess."

Sarina's magnificent eyes suddenly rimmed with tears. "Why are you so cruel?"

"Won't work, Mum. You'd remember him. Tjungurra?"

Sarina didn't say anything for a moment. She looked mystified.

"The old witch doctor, the *kurdaitcha* man," Mel prompted.

"That old cannibal, looking for *me?"* Sarina asked in

amazement. "Whatever for? I never had anything to do with such a creature."

"Well, he's come looking for you," Mel said. "Heard the old lion is dead. Michael is dead. There's only *you*. I even had a bit of a scare. He thought I *was* you."

Sarina took a sharp breath. "Well, you certainly look like me." She put up her hands, rubbing her fingers across her temples. "What is this?" She appeared genuinely bewildered. But who would know? Her mother might be one of the greatest actresses in the world, but Mel's gut instinct told her that she really didn't know.

"It's a good thing you're getting out of here, Mum," she said. "You're hated. The evil old bird even came in ritual dress. I believe he was responsible for the stampede that killed Michael. It would be easy for him. He was over twenty years younger. I further believe Mireille put him up to it. She was in league with the devil. Langdon was too powerful to touch. You were locked away in the homestead, pretty well inaccessible. Easy to lie in wait for Michael. Your shocking affair with Gregory Langdon led to an innocent man's death," she cried in fierce and passionate challenge.

Sarina suddenly appeared massively uneasy. "Sheer speculation! You always did have an over-vivid imagination, Amelia."

"*I* have?" Mel cried. "That's rich, coming from you."

"I know absolutely nothing about this," Sarina swore. "It's not even something I can accept. Michael's death was investigated. It was a tragic accident."

Mel shook her head. "Mireille and Tjungurra were in it together."

Sarina bristled with anger. "Where's the proof? You're a sad, disturbed soul, Amelia."

"I have been, but not any more. I've been the victim of a conspiracy."

Sarina reacted with fury. "This is bizarre! I would *never* have been party to having Michael harmed. He was a good man, good to me. He helped me get away."

"But he wasn't my father?"

Colour rose to Sarina's face. "No, Amelia, I've told you he wasn't."

That hit her like a body blow.

Sarina spoke as though she had at long last laid down a heavy burden. "Michael came to my rescue after my lover abandoned me. The man promised me he was going to leave his wife. He swore he loved me. Never, ever believe a man loves you, Amelia. He may lust after you. *Love,* never. My father and my lover were responsible for what happened to me. I hate men. They're users. They can discard women like old shoes. Women don't matter. He gave me money instead."

Mel tried very hard to keep calm. "So the burning question—who *was* he?"

"Let me finish." Sarina had to gulp for air. "He was much respected in the town. A science teacher. I was a schoolgirl. He used to give me a ride home sometimes from school. Such a gentleman."

Mel couldn't answer for a moment, then she said, "Mum, I can't bear to hear. Just tell me the name of the town. I'll find out, anyway. Don't make an enemy of me. You've got enough already. Wonder of wonders, I'm still an ally."

"You *are* my daughter," Sarina reminded Mel with monumental self-regard. "The name of the town is Silverton."

Mel didn't have a clue. "Am I supposed to know where that is?"

"North Queensland." Sarina rested her head in her hands.

Mel took a deep breath, trying to shake off her feeling of unreality. "But you always said your family lived in Sydney, thousands of miles away from North Queensland."

Sarina gave a sour laugh. "I was more comfortable with Sydney, that's all. Love hurts, Amelia."

"Everything hurts!" Mel burst out. "Love kills. Betrayal kills. It killed Michael. And Mireille was prepared to have it done. But *you* were the one who exposed him to danger."

Sarina swept to her feet, a twisted smile on her beautiful face. "I expect God will punish me. That's if there is one. I don't think highly of myself, Amelia. I am what I am."

"Mum, anyone could say that. But you say it as though your actions can't be explained otherwise. I suppose you couldn't really love me because I was *that* man's child. The man who abandoned you. So you're what, Mum—forty-three, forty-four?"

"Something like that." Sarina looked away. "Beauty can be a curse, Amelia. A curse when you're young. A curse as you age and begin to suffer the ravages of time."

"Well, that hasn't happened to you so far, Mum," Mel said acidly. "You look terrific and hey, you're rich!"

Sarina walked to the door and leaned a hand against it for support. "Don't go looking for that man, Amelia," she warned. "I can spare you that, at least. He won't want to know you if he's even alive. He was nearly twice my age then. He laid waste to my youth, to my life. My own father did the rest." Sarina spoke with so much passion she might have been re-living that traumatic time.

"Secrets, secrets, you've guarded them well. Your family lived in Silverton. It's probably where you met Michael. And what of my grandparents?"

"They were punished," said Sarina, her normally dulcet tones as hard as flint.

Mel got a grip on her mother's shoulder. "Punished, how?"

"They're dead, Amelia. Killed in a car crash."

A doubting voice inside Mel's head kicked in. "Did that just pop into your mind? I'm going to check all this out, Mum. I'm sorry for what happened to you. You were little more than a child. It was way too soon to have a baby. But you could have been a good mother to me—instead, you turned your back."

Sarina continued to lean her hand against the door. "How could I comfort you, when I was in desperate need of comfort myself?"

Mel nodded, trying very hard to understand. "Tell me, did you love Gregory Langdon or did you simply use him?"

"He was mesmerized by me," Sarina said, straightening and throwing up her head like a movie queen. "I grew to have strong feelings for him, but, yes, I used him at first to accomplish my goal. Poor Michael aside, I'd have done anything to avenge myself on men. They betray us. Dev is a far, far better man than Gregory could ever have been, but he won't marry you, Amelia. Listen, because I'm only trying to save you."

"Too late, Mum. Neither Dev nor I seem able to let go."

"Are you mad, then?" Sarina rounded on her daughter, great eyes flashing. "You've been warned. In the end you'll find your dreams will dissolve. *Just like mine.*"

Great clumps of fiery red earth clustered with wild flowers, were thrown up as the mare's hoofs thundered across the desert plains. The eroded hills in the distance glowed a salmon pink. By high noon they would have warmed to cinnabar, then furnace-red, heralding a glorious rose-gold sunset. The great prehistoric monuments of the Red Centre underwent spectacular colour changes during the course of a day. Uluru, venerated by the Lorijitas and known to them as *Oolera,* was a sacred dreaming place created by the all-powerful spirits. It rosé over a thousand feet above the desert sands with the great mass of it buried below the sands, a single mighty boulder, the largest monolith in the world. Farther away rose the Olgas, Kata Tjunta, with its fascinating domes and turrets.

Gradually Mel calmed. Silhouetted darkly above her head a lone wedge-tailed eagle was performing its daily ritual, wheeling in higher and higher semicircles. The eagle was sacred to the desert tribes. The budgerigar accompanied her on her ride, clouds of parrot green and gold. She carried the wild beauty of Kooraki, the immensity of it, in her soul. The mare was heading almost of its own accord towards one of the most beautiful lagoons on the station and Kooraki boasted a great many. The waters, the darkest green of a rainforest, some turquoise-sheened, floated cargoes of exquisite water lilies all year round. Each lagoon, pond, billabong and swamp on the station carried its lovely flotilla generally of a single colour—the sacred blue lotus, pink, cream, white or yellow, the stunning blooms rising above their thick green pads. They made a heart-stirring sight.

At the top of the acacia-lined bank she tethered the mare, then half walked, half skittered down the slope, crushing pretty little purple plants almost flush with the soil underfoot. With a final leap, she came down on the pale ochre sand that formed a broad beach around the deep lagoon. Here the sacred blue lotus decorated the lagoon's reed-shadowed borders. Many a time she and Dev had made love in the cool green shadows to the back of her, sheltered by the overhanging feathery boughs of the acacias, heavy in golden blossom and scent. Their coming together right from the very first time had been as natural as life itself.

Dev crouching over her...kissing her...caressing her... Even thinking about it now rocked her body with sensations. Dev was a fantastic lover. Once he had told her his feeling of rapture was so intense he could die from it. She had felt the same way. Dev was her soul, boy and man. He had shaped all the days of her life. She knew she could never love anyone again who was not Dev.

Only what had he done with wicked old Tjungurra?

She knew he wasn't going to deliver the old witch doctor to the police. Blood was thicker than water. Dev was a Langdon. His first loyalty would be to his family, even to the memory of his dreadful grandmother.

Mel sank on the sand and softly wept. The thought of Michael and the manner of his dying had haunted her for years. Never in a million light years would she have suspected the old *kurdaitcha* man of playing a part in Michael's tragic "accident." The fact that the old man had turned up had seriously rattled her faith in Dev. At some stage Tjungurra must have been considered. He had been treated with a mixture of reverence and fear. But both she and Dev had been children at the time. Now, years later? Had someone confided their suspicions to Dev? It could even have been his grandfather who'd had to deal with the fallout and a raging wife half off her head with jealousy. It was a huge comfort that her mother had no idea. Sarina had genuinely cared about Michael as being the man apart.

Her breath was coming ragged in her throat. The breeze dried her tears. It was like silk against her flushed skin. For long moments she stared at the wide glittering expanse of water, the surface as smooth as poured glass. There was no one around for miles. The men would be working at the Ten Mile. A dip would cool her off and soothe her frazzled nerves.

She stood up, stripping off her clothes until she was down to her bra and briefs. She had to get on with life. She had to go in search of her biological father. *Silverton.* It wasn't one of the big sugar towns. She had a vague idea the district was a producer of tropical fruit, mango plantations. Sarina wasn't the first love-struck teenager to fall in love with a much older man, married or not. She would track this man down. Maybe give him one hell of a fright, she looked so much like Sarina, the young girl he had abandoned.

The lagoon beckoned. Though the sun was hot, the water

was surprisingly cold. Bending her supple body, she splashed her face, her arms and her breasts, before diving in. She swam well. As a girl, she had won many medals for her school in the inter-schools swimming contests. Gregory Langdon had paid for her excellent education at one of the country's top girls' schools.

Thank you, Gregory, you old tyrant.

She felt no gratitude. Only shame.

Dev found her lying on the sand, half asleep. Her breathing was shallow but relaxed. God, she was beautiful. He stood for a time watching her. But when he allowed his shadow to fall over her, her eyes flew open, hand up, shading them, as she gave a soft exclamation.

"How long have you been standing there?" she asked with a frown, starting to sit up.

"Just arrived," he said laconically. "Enjoy your swim?"

"It helped." Mel drew up her long slender legs, hugging her knees. God knew, Dev was intimate with her naked body, yet as his jewellike eyes smouldered and touched on different places she felt a hard knot of desire beginning to twist and twirl around inside her.

Only nothing romantic was about to happen. Not after the shattering events of that morning.

"So what did you do with your old witch doctor?" she challenged, looking straight at him.

"Standard thing. Killed him." Dev lowered his lean length to the sand beside her.

"Your grandmother had Michael killed," she said bleakly. "How do you feel about that?"

He turned to touch her face. "Heavy-hearted, Mel, if it were true."

"Another one of my quantum leaps?" she asked bitterly.

"Your antennae could be way off. The old man frightened the life out of the stable lads. They were terrified."

"I saw that," she said shortly. "What was he jabbering about, anyway? I did catch one word—*Sarina.*"

"Apparently he thought you were her," Dev told her with a sharp exhalation of breath. "He tells me he's dying."

"Good!" Mel exclaimed at once. "He must be a thousand years old anyway. How many times did he see Sarina? He never came anywhere near the house. Sure he didn't come seeking redemption? Or did he plan to plunge his spear-thrower into the heart of that wicked unfaithful woman?"

"Mel, Tjungurra has come back to Kooraki to *die.* He would be hard-pressed to fight off a child, let alone sink his spear in anyone. His long walkabout took what remaining strength he had from his body."

"So you're saying you're going to allow him to die on Kooraki?" she asked in angry disbelief.

"That's what I'm saying, Mel." His tone firmed. "This is Tjungurra's ancestral land. His tribe was here tens of thousands of years before the white man arrived. He'll do no one any harm, be certain of that. His people will help ease him out of life. He faces judgement, too, Mel. I think he's scared he won't make his way up to the stars. All Aboriginals are stargazers."

"We share that, don't we?" She cast him another challenging look. "How many times did we lie staring up at the stars, you filling my head with stories about Orion, the mighty hunter with his jewelled belt, the marvel of the Milky Way, that great river of stars, home of all those who lead good lives? That leaves quite a few people we know out. You were the one to show me the pointers to the Cross, Beta Centari, Alpha Centari. You shared all the stories you'd learned from the Aboriginals about our constellation. Your mother used to wear a very beautiful jewelled brooch representing the Southern Cross."

Dev nodded. "I remember it. Each jewel was different—a diamond, a sapphire, a ruby and an emerald. Dad gave it to her when they were courting."

"They never had their own life, did they?" she lamented. "Your father should have moved you all away."

"He was trapped, Mel. Can't you understand that? He was the heir. He was convinced his first duty was to Grandfather, which was to say Kooraki."

"And boy, didn't he suffer!" Mel exclaimed dismally. "Your mother. Ava, too. You managed to keep above it all but even you had endless fights with your grandfather. I know better than to ask you what the last big fight was about." No stopping the bitterness.

"Seriously, Mel, you wouldn't want to know. It was rubbish, anyway." Dev's expression had grown taut, his mood edgy.

"So, I don't get the chance to decide that for myself. Impossible to keep my mother out of it. I'm not a fool, Dev." Mel stood up, reaching for her jeans. She stepped into them, zipping them up.

Dev held her cotton shirt in his hand. "What a beautiful body you have."

"Shirt, please." There was a great brittleness to her movements.

He passed it to her without another word. She didn't bother tucking it in.

Dev raked a hand through his tousled blond waves. They blended in with the golden sunlight. "What more did you manage to get out of your mother?" he asked abruptly.

"More? What gives you that idea?"

"You're keeping something from me. I know you, Mel."

She pulled her thick mane out of its topknot, shaking it

loose. "Imagine that! You can keep things back. I can't." She stared out over the glittering water, where iridescent winged creatures were whirring before taking flight again.

Dev didn't respond as she expected, but when she turned her head to look at him, his hand shot out to encircle her arm. "Keep still," he murmured.

She obeyed without question. The reason for his action was immediately apparent. A pair of brolgas, the Australian blue cranes, long-legged, long-necked, were coming in to land on the sandy beach of the opposite bank. They bounced lightly, elegantly.

Mel drew in her breath, seizing on this rare moment of peace. "How about that?" she breathed.

"Sit down, Mel," he urged. "This is a privilege we can never take for granted."

She sank onto the warm sand beside him. Maybe this was a good omen. One couldn't survive without hope.

Within moments the taller brolga, close on five feet with the identifying scarlet patch across its face, bowed, grey wings with darker wing tips outstretched, waiting on its mate to bow gracefully in return. This was the start of the celebrated brolga ceremonial dance.

Mel bypassed the tension that was strung out between them. She reacted in the way she had done since childhood. She put out her hand, feeling Dev's close warmly around hers. They sat in silence, watching the birds begin their famous courting ritual of wonderful vertical leaps, amazing side steps, graceful dips. It was quite extraordinary, the rituals of nature, the wildlife, the beauty and mystery of it all.

The dance gradually came to an end. They would have applauded, only they knew they would startle the cranes and the wealth of bird life that was all but invisible in the blossoming trees.

"Peace does exist," Dev said very quietly. "Even if it's sometimes hard to find. How beautiful is our world!"

She acknowledged it. "I love it as much as you do. If only we could start over."

Dev shook his head. "Impossible. We have to take whatever life hands out. You know my view. There's no point expending time and energy on regrets for the past. We live in the present. We look to the future. Only way to go."

"I've never been as secure as you."

He lay his hand with tenderness against her hot, flushed cheek. "All this torment has been bound up with your mother, but she's off our hands."

Mel felt the bitter taste of that on her tongue. "You won't believe what she had to say."

"Try me." His voice took on a hard edge. "I knew it was something."

Mel picked up a lovely coral-pink shell that was half embedded in the sand. "That dear man, Michael Norton, wasn't my father." Her beautiful face poignantly expressed her sorrow.

After the initial shock, Dev wasn't all that surprised. "I'm sorry, Mel. I can feel your pain. But go on."

Mel calmed herself. "It still hasn't sunk in. My mother claims to have fallen pregnant to a married man, her teacher, when she was still at school. You can imagine how beautiful she was. He took advantage of her. Her family turned against her, her father especially. They disowned her. Or so she says. I can never completely believe my mother. Not when she's undergone a metamorphosis right in front of my eyes. But life *has* damaged her. Her home town was Silverton. Heard of it?"

Dev shot her a frowning look. "Of course I've heard of it. It's a prosperous little town in far North Queensland— processed dried fruit, mango plantations. That's probably where she met Mike. He came to us from Maru Downs. Silverton would be one of the closest towns to the station."

Mel took a hard swallow. "I'd always believed her people were in Sydney, with its huge Italian population."

"Your mother obviously found it easier to lie," Dev said. "There's a sizeable Italian population in North Queensland. Our sugar industry owes a great debt to immigrant Italian families. They were the ones who worked the sugar farms, then saved up to buy them."

Mel waited until she could speak properly, her mouth was so dry. "Revelations have been raining down on me like chunks of debris from out of space."

Dev's response was to nod slowly. "And her parents, your grandparents?"

Mel couldn't answer for a moment. "Dead in a car crash," she managed with stark finality. "Sarina doesn't mourn them." She found it too distressing to mention the accusation Sarina had brought against her father. She couldn't bear to think about it herself. Sarina could well be delusional.

Dev's face registered his scepticism. "Hasn't Sarina taken an age telling you all this?" He spoke with harsh condemnation.

"I don't think she would have told me at all, only I unnerved her saying the old witch doctor was after her. I'm convinced from her reaction she knew nothing of any conspiracy against Michael."

"If there *was* one." Dev cut her off. "We'll never know, Mel. We weren't the main players. We were kids. We have to strive to put it behind us."

"Easier said than done," Mel answered, finding recovery difficult. Why don't you turn the wicked old devil over to the police?"

"On what charge?"

Her mind raced. "You don't believe your grandmother

could have been a part of it? She said many terrible things to me. You know that. I told you everything that ever really mattered. Easy for her to enlist Tjungurra's help."

"No, I won't have it. She wasn't *that* bad. And she had a right to be jealous. Anyway, they're gone, Mel, my grandparents." He picked up a small round stone, then sent it skittering across the surface of the water. "Sarina was the catalyst. Condemn *her* along with the rest." Because of Sarina, he never did get the chance to say goodbye to his grandfather, a giant in his life. Sarina was a woman who had seduction in her very nature. A man's admiration was pure oxygen to her.

"So what are we left with?" Mel was demanding to know.

"Some answers never come, Mel. Bitterness is a sickness, a cancer. It eats its way through us. My grandfather wanted Sarina madly. Who knows if it was love or not? It was certainly lust. My grandmother lived with hatred. Mike Norton was caught in Sarina's web, too much in love with her to anger her with questions. Did he know he wasn't your father?"

Mel felt a wave of grief. "How would I know? My mother only feeds you slivers at a time. All I do know is he loved *me*."

"Of course he did!" Dev said, conviction in his voice. "I was only a boy but I still remember how Mike adored his astonishingly pretty little princess. Maybe your mother told him, maybe she didn't. Lies and the truth are as one with her. We've both seen her reinvent herself, literally overnight. It could *all* be fantasy."

"Which is why I'm going to check it out," Mel said with determination.

"Go to Silverton?"

Mel ran a finger over her aching forehead. "Yes."

Dev didn't hesitate. "I'll take you, even if it is a wild goose chase. But if Sarina lived there, someone will know. Her face alone is a standout. She might well have been using a false name. It wouldn't surprise me."

"Me, neither," Mel confessed, remembering the odd things her mother had said. "I think the trauma of having me so young, so unsupported by family, could have turned her mind. The experience made her incapable of feeling compassion for others. She didn't receive it. She didn't give it. Who am I to judge her?"

"Before you get too forgiving, Mel, you might remember, she went to work on my grandfather. She would have been sending out messages, the great dark eyes, the subtle nuances in the voice. She used her beauty. She knew he was a married man. But she thrust that aside as of little consequence. Most people would side with my grandmother, even if she didn't handle the situation at all well."

"That's why she enlisted the old *kurdaitcha* man's help," Mel insisted, causing Dev to groan.

"A *theory,* Mel, based on the fact the old man turned up again."

"To die?" She didn't doubt he was dying, but what else had he come for?

"That's what he said."

"And that's what you accepted." Mel looked out over the lagoon, where the water was so clear and pure one could drink it. "Why wouldn't you cover up for your grandmother? Too late to do anything about the old man. He'd perish within a day in jail."

"You know he would."

"So you're offering to fly me to Maru Downs?"

"Fly us to Maru. Anything to get you to move forward, Mel," he said tersely.

The expression in Mel's eyes turned cool. "I can only do that when I can separate the truth from the lies. Surely that makes sense?"

"Something has to." Dev's response was weary.

Mel stood up, then began to button up her cotton shirt.

As he looked at her, violent sensations rushed through him. He knew if he pulled her to him he wouldn't be able to stop. Mel belonged to him. And he to her. "It might take a day or two to organise it."

"Fine." Tears sprang into her eyes.

"Mel! Your tears can break my heart in an instant." He reached out then, cupping a hand around her nape, kissing her with his open mouth. He threw everything of himself into it, feeling, after a mere moment of resistance, her tongue mating with his in the eternal dance of love. The places a tongue could go! The places Mel had learned from him. He couldn't bear to think Mel could be right about Tjungurra. The charge was too serious to walk away from, but there was little choice. They both had to walk away from it.

Mel broke the kiss, resting her face against his neck.

"Everything is going to be different, Mel," he promised her. "Better."

"It would be too terrifying to think otherwise." She slowly pulled away. "Are you going back to the house?"

"I have to. Patrick O'Hare will be here for lunch. He has a business proposition he wants to put to me. He and my grandfather had quite a few things going together."

Mel knew that for a fact. She took a long breath, keeping her tone neutral. "I'd be surprised if he comes alone. Siobhan will tag along. Hope burns bright. It glitters like gold. Siobhan won't miss an opportunity to see you."

"Don't start, Mel." Dev jerked his blond head up impatiently. "Siobhan is easy enough company. I hope you're going to join us."

"Of course." Mel was seized with shame that she had felt such a violent pang of jealousy.

Dev's voice roused her. "O'Hare has been after Illuka for

quite a while." He named a Langdon outstation. "I'll sell for the right price." He knew Mel was spot on about pretty little Siobhan and her hopes. She did fancy herself in love with him, her hopes buoyed by her parents' wholehearted support for a union between the two families. Strangely, or perhaps not so strangely, Siobhan had never mentioned the bond everyone knew existed between him and Mel. Maybe Siobhan had allowed herself to believe that bond was platonic, not sexual. A cousinly sort of thing. He disliked the whole concept of matchmaking. He had never given Siobhan any reason for hope. It had been friendship all the way.

CHAPTER EIGHT

SIOBHAN O'HARE made a special effort to look her best for her trip to Kooraki with her father. Her father, needless to say, was only too pleased to take her. Both parents, her mother especially, entertained hopes that she might, if she hung in there, land arguably the most eligible bachelor in the country— James Devereaux Langdon. She and Dev had always been friends, and at not that far off thirty it was high time Dev took a wife. Plenty of eligible young women were standing in line—she was the closest geographically, at least—Dev had only to make a decision. Now that he had stepped into Gregory Langdon's shoes, there was extra pressure on Dev to marry and have a family, hopefully sons to run the Langdon cattle empire.

She had a big advantage, being Outback born and bred and a member of the O'Hare pioneering family, with its proud history. She had hoped, prayed, finally convinced herself she had as good a chance as anyone. There *was* that persistent niggle at the back of her mind. Her mother felt it, too. That niggle was Amelia Norton. One had to be realistic. Amelia was a very beautiful young woman, exotic and astonishingly beautiful. That was her Italian blood. She even had an intensely attractive voice and a beguiling way with her hands, little turns of the wrists and upraised splayed fingers. Her Italian blood again. Not only that, she was clever. She held down a top job with a leading investment bank.

The big turn-off was the mother, the former housekeeper who overnight had become a rich woman. It was now apparent to everyone that Sarina Norton had been Gregory Langdon's mistress. No one seemed prepared to forgive or forget that. There could be a public scandal looming if anyone leaked information to the press. Her family never would. They were trusted friends. She knew there was a strong bond between Dev and Amelia, but surely it was almost like *family?* In no way did Dev and Amelia act like lovers. That gave her heart hope. Their behaviour was more like affectionate bantering, sparring cousins. Still, the strong connection was there. Given the chance, she would sound Amelia out.

Just as Mel had predicted, Siobhan arrived with her father. Both father and daughter greeted Mel warmly, though an indefinable light shone in Siobhan's bright blue eyes. She was looking extremely pretty. Her short copper curls glittered in the sunlight. Her soft fair skin was lightly peppered with freckles across her pert nose. She wore a very becoming white linen dress, sleeveless, round necked with circular medallions of cotton lace and crewel work adorning the skirt. When Dev bent to kiss her cheek she held up a rapt face like a flower to the sun, her hand involuntarily stroking his arm.

Siobhan in the sunlight! All light and white petunia skin. She was smiling at Dev in a way that made Mel's heart ache. Dev wasn't in love with Siobhan. But it was there for anyone to see—Siobhan was head over heels in love with Dev. Such a marvellous feeling to be in love, Mel thought with a twist of the heart. Hell to be in love with the wrong man. The O'Hares were good people, much respected in the vast Outback community. Siobhan was blessed. She enjoyed ap-

proval all round. She was much loved by her parents. That
alone was a priceless gift, in Mel's view.

Lunch was served in the cool of the loggia that looked out
over the rear landscaped gardens and the turquoise swimming pool with its beautiful mosaic tiles. A poolside pergola
was a short distance away, with cushioned banquettes and a
long, low timber table. Mel had often eaten a breakfast of
tropical fruit there.

Her mother's former second in charge, now elevated to the
position of housekeeper, Nula Morris, was proving her ef-
ficiency by serving and presenting a light, delicious meal of
chilled avocado, lime and cilantro soup. It was followed by
sweet-and-sour seafood salad that had its origin in Thailand.
Her mother had often served Thai dishes, mainly because
Gregory Langdon had loved them. A coconut and ginger ice
cream garnished with mint sprigs had been made to end the
meal if anyone wanted a scoop or two. Mel was the only one
to decline. She had eaten with little enthusiasm. She didn't
have much of an appetite these days.

Over lunch Siobhan came alive. Pretty face thrown up,
riding high, she broke completely free of her usual shyness
around Dev to sparkle. She launched into a stream of funny
stories and gossip that made them all laugh. That clearly delighted her. Siobhan had a talent for mimicry that added to
the comic effect. Her father smiled on her proudly. His little
girl, wasn't she wonderful? Dev, too, was looking at her with
easy affection, something that must have gladdened the heart
of both daughter and father. Mel tried to capture some of the
mood. She was fully aware of Dev's sharpening attention on
her, the *watchfulness* behind the white smiles. Tension continued to burn slowly between them like a fuse.

Mel tormented herself with a visual image. Dev and a radiant Siobhan standing before an altar, Siobhan in the love-

liest of satin and lace wedding gowns, a short starburst of tulle around her head, a posy of white and cream roses in her hand. Every woman wished and prayed for happiness in love. Oh, to find it in marriage to that one man, a soulmate! That was the way things should be. The sad reality was that many chose the wrong man and lived to regret it.

Afterwards the men withdrew to Dev's study to talk business, leaving the two young women alone. Mel thought it might be a good idea to retain a little distance between herself and Siobhan, only Siobhan had other ideas.

They were strolling in the garden, heading in the direction of the bougainvillea-wreathed arcade. "So when are you thinking of heading back to Sydney?" Siobhan asked, linking her arm through Mel's in a gesture of friendship, but really settling into an interrogation of sorts.

"I'm not exactly sure," Mel replied, well aware that Siobhan was trying to pick up signals.

"It must be hard for you, Amelia, coping?"

Her approach angered Mel but she kept calm. Unhurriedly, she withdrew her arm, pretending she wanted to study the huge yellow and scarlet spikes of the Kahili Ginger Blossom. It might have been a rare plant instead of one that thrived in the garden. "Coping with what?" Mel asked, keeping moving.

Siobhan wasn't to be put off, her gentle voice gathering strength. "This business about your mother," she said. "We all feel for you, Amelia." She began to describe circles in the air that apparently denoted "feeling."

"Why should you think I need your kind feelings, Siobhan?"

Siobhan's petunia-petal skin coloured up. "I just wanted you to know you have *friends.*"

Mel considered that. "I do have friends, but that's nice of you, Siobhan."

"Oh, that's all right," Siobhan answered with a smile.

"I should tell you I have all the friends I need."

Siobhan made a funny little sound of distress. "There, I've upset you. But you don't need *enemies,* Amelia, because of your mother. All those noughts!" she exclaimed. "Twenty million dollars wasn't it?"

Mel came to a halt, her passionate face betraying her anger, her great dark eyes on fire. "Who told you?"

Siobhan's stomach gave a downward lunge. She took a hasty step back, replying in a voice of soft amazement. "Why Dev, of course."

"Not true!" Mel flatly contradicted. As petite Siobhan moved back she took a step closer.

Siobhan gave a nervous laugh. "Would I lie to you?"

Mel brushed that aside. "You just did. I think you're anxious to help me on my way, Siobhan. I know you feel deeply for Dev."

Siobhan blushed scarlet. "Is it that apparent?"

"It is to me. I don't blame you in the least. Dev is an extremely handsome and charismatic man. So what is it that's worrying you about *me?*"

Siobhan looked highly uncomfortable, shrugging her delicate shoulders. "I need to find out the lay of the land. You and Dev are close. Everyone knows that. You always have been."

"You have difficulty with it?"

"No, no!" Siobhan protested breathlessly. "I understand. You were a very lonely child. No friends of your own, your mother the housekeeper. Dev must have been your knight in shining armour."

"And you wish to know if he still is?" Mel asked bluntly.

Siobhan pulled her pert features into an expression of apology.

"Give it to me straight, Siobhan," Mel advised. "You want to know if Dev and I have a sexual relationship? Is that it? You want to know if there's any chance it might come to something?"

Siobhan pulled back contritely. "Please, Amelia, I have no wish to upset you."

"Then why bring up the subject?"

"Apologies, apologies! You're someone I really admire, Amelia. You're so beautiful." Privately, she and her mother were in agreement that Amelia could do something to tone down her sexuality. "And you're *clever*. Dev is forever singing your praises. I just wanted to know if I had a chance with him, that's all."

Mel waited while Siobhan had her say. "That's *all?* That's a *lot* to know, Siobhan. Why don't you ask *Dev,* not me?"

Siobhan's pretty face was shocked. "I'm not good at that sort of thing. Much too forward. I thought you might help me as a sort of favour. I've always liked you. So do my parents. We've always felt sorry for you."

"So you keep running past me," Mel said shortly. "I'm in no need of your pity, Siobhan. I do very well. You, on the other hand, might consider this. *Lies* are easy to tell but very difficult to make right. Dev *didn't* tell you how much Gregory Langdon left my mother."

Siobhan's pretty face wore a look of guilt. She waved her two hands in front of her face without answering.

"That doesn't tell me much," Mel said.

"He might have told Dad," Siobhan mumbled, digging herself further in. Put on the spot, she found she couldn't admit to anything bad about herself.

Mel relented. "I accept your family has high hopes for a union between your two families, Siobhan. I expect you're getting plenty of loving but constant pressure from your parents to bring that about. It would be considered a tremendous coup."

Proudly, Siobhan threw up her copper head. "Is that so dreadful? Should I be defending our family position? I've had a huge crush on Dev since I was a girl," she proclaimed, her voice rising. "I know he's very fond of me. If you're not in the picture in that way, Amelia—I fully accept your long friendship with Dev—I feel I have a chance with Dev. There's no one else on the scene, as far as I know. Megan Kennedy couldn't hold him and she sure tried hard enough. She told me Dev was dynamite in bed."

Mel felt a dull roar in her ears. "How massively indiscreet everyone has become these days. Personally, I don't believe in kiss-and-tell. But you're in no position to second Megan's opinion."

Siobhan coloured up violently. "No, no! But Dev has to marry soon. It's expected of him. Especially now." Siobhan's expression was contrite. "You must surely understand?"

Mel stared away across the garden to the calm, dark, green waters of a man-made pond. It was so beautiful, densely framed by pristine white arum lilies, with their lush green foliage and a spectacular jostling of purple flowering water plants deeper into the bog. "I do, Siobhan," she said quietly.

"Oh, that's great!" Siobhan spoke as if a huge weight had been lifted from her shoulders. "You won't give me away, will you? I mean, you won't tell Dev about our conversation?"

"Of course not," Mel said. "This is private and it will remain that way. Good thing I'm not Megan Kennedy. Don't get *too* optimistic, Siobhan," she warned.

"I won't." Siobhan nodded, as though heeding good advice. "I mean, Dev's only just lost his grandfather. He would have trouble thinking about marriage right at this point."

"Perhaps he's already made up his mind," said Mel.

Siobhan pinked up again. "Maybe he has," she said with a hopeful smile, her blue eyes full of twinkling lights.

All Mel felt was emotionally drained. Her mother's parting words resounded in her ears.

In the end you'll find your dreams will dissolve. Just like mine.

Patrick O'Hare had flown over to Kooraki in his yellow bumblebee of a helicopter. Business matters concluded to both men's satisfaction, father and daughter made their farewells. Siobhan hugged Mel, grasping the taller Mel close as if they were new best friends.

"We must stay in touch, Amelia." She smiled jauntily, as though at long last she had gained some sort of an ascendancy over Mel. "Mum and I often go to Sydney or Melbourne to do our shopping or take in a show. I'd like to give you a call when I'm in Sydney." She looked to Mel for confirmation.

"Please do." What else could she say? Please *don't?*

Dev was driving father and daughter down to the airstrip. They were seated in the Jeep and before Dev climbed on board he turned back for a word with Mel. "I'll be back," he advised in a voice that suggested she might take it into her head to hop in a Jeep and tear off to the Simpson Desert.

"What's the panic? I'm not going anywhere."

He gave her a taut version of his white smile. "Not yet."

"I have an investigation to attend to, Dev," Mel said.

"And I'm going to help you. I thought we'd agreed on that," Dev responded tersely, rubbing his cleft chin. "You don't have to go it alone. Whatever the true story is, Mel, there's bound to be fallout."

"I'm prepared for it," she said firmly. "For all we know, my mother's windfall might soon make the papers."

"A nine-day wonder," Dev pronounced. "Your mother's

latest version of her life story mightn't be the final one. There could be yet another draft," he warned. Sarina Norton was definitely damaged.

"That's what we have to find out. Did Michael have family?"

"It would have been checked out at the time. No one, as far as I know, turned up for the funeral."

"I wish I'd been much older," said Mel, a thousand regrets rising to her mind. "I'd have known so much *more,* instead of being kept in the dark. You'd better go," she said sweetly. "Siobhan is looking anxious."

"Funning, are you?" Dev clipped off. "Just be here when I get back."

It was a good fifteen minutes before Dev returned. He found Mel in the library. "The good news is O'Hare is willing to meet my price for Illuka," he said, slumping, albeit elegantly, into a wing-backed chair.

"And the bad news?"

"Well, I don't know if it's *bad,* exactly," he teased, "but Siobhan gave me an epic hug and a kiss goodbye."

"Lucky you." Mel closed the book she had taken down from a shelf, a signed copy of Patrick White's *The Tree of Man,* set in the Australian wilderness. It had contributed to his winning the Nobel Prize back in 1973. The Nobel committee commented that White had "introduced a new continent into literature." Australia, the oldest continent on earth. Mel had read and re-read the book. She never tired of it. "A sea change appears to have come over our Siobhan lately," she observed.

"Yes, indeed. I've never heard her so chatty."

"Put her out of her misery, Dev," she advised. With his iridescent eyes on her, her heart was starting to beat high in her chest.

Dev continued on his way. "It's the Celt in her. Makes her unpredictable."

"And she's upping her game."

"Then she's peaked way too fast," Dev said sardonically, eyeing Mel as she sat at the circular library table. She was wearing a simple white ribbed singlet that set off her golden skin, paired with black linen chinos, a tan leather belt slung around her narrow waist. Mel always did look great in whatever she wore. Definitely not your girl next door.

"I have to fly to Sydney Monday next," he told her.

"Business?" Mel looked across at him. Dev would be expecting far more of it.

He gave a faint sigh. "Always business. I need to call in on one of Granddad's stockbrokers. Want to come?"

"Not if it delays my trip to Silverton," she answered. "I can find the town by myself."

"Sure you can, but I can make your journey easy and safe. I don't like the idea of your haring around the bush by yourself. It's still frontier country, Mel. Sydney first, then Silverton right after. How's that?"

She took her time to reply. "I guess I'm happy enough with that."

He gave a satirical whoop. "*You're* happy, *I'm* happy. Hallelujah!" He stood up purposefully, as though he had wasted enough time. "Why don't you come on down with me to the Five Mile? We're shifting a big mob into a holding hard. We could do with some help. Some of the boys are still out in the desert rounding up strays and any cleanskins they can find. We'll divide the cleanskins with Patrick O'Hare. The trouble is, cattle split up as they graze and a lot go missing each year. Just roaming wild. They love it."

"Freedom," Mel said. "We *all* love it. I'll need to change. Give me half an hour. I'll join you."

"Great! Thank God I can trust you not to lose yourself!"

Dev rested a hand on her shoulder as he passed her chair. "I've lost count of the number of warnings I've had to issue to visitors over the years. Remember the guy who told me he utilized the eeny, meeney, miny, moe set of coordinates?"

Mel had to laugh. "That was the polo player, wasn't it, Chris Quentin?" A search party had been organized to find him. She had been part of it.

Dev sighed. "Not much good in the bush, old Chris. He was probably just riding along thinking of *you*. It was getting to the stage where I thought he was going to ask for permission to marry you."

"How do you know I wasn't tempted to say yes?"

Dev gave a spluttering laugh. "Ah, come on, Mel," he mocked. "You're addicted to *me*. I'm the same with you." The mockery in his voice deepened. "You're my favourite woman in the whole wide world, no matter how many Stop signs you've erected along the way. I bet you wouldn't swear to obey me until death—or divorce—us do part."

The thought shook her. "Langdons didn't believe in divorce," she retorted.

"Not so far. Looks like Ava is set to make history." His expression sobered. "Of all the guys she could have chosen, why *him*?"

"We both know Ava saw her marriage as an escape."

"Who could blame her?" Dev sighed. "God, you were the most gorgeous bridesmaid. Extravagantly beautiful." Ava had four very good-looking bridesmaids in attendance for her wedding, two blondes, two brunettes. Mel had been maid of honour. The bold colours of their dresses had been a talking point. Ava had borrowed them from her favourite flower, the tulip—a fabulous deep purple, an intense pink, a dark crimson and a richly glowing amber. With such strong blocks of colour, one might have thought they would clash but they had looked luscious. "Whatever happened to that amber dress?" he asked.

"I've still got it. I did look good in it, didn't I? But no way did I trump Ava. No bride could have looked lovelier."

"Perfect foils," said Dev, the best memories of that day still clear in his mind. "Now, I'm outta here. You might take Gunner. He could do with a ride."

"Right!" Gunner, with studbook blood, was a chestnut gelding who she had found to her delight could do tricks. She was happy to be put to work. That way she wouldn't have time to *think*. Maybe when she was out on the vast empty plains she might see the ghost of the gentle man she had called *"Daddy."* Michael Norton had been a good man. She would remember him with great affection mixed with sadness all the days of her life.

By the time Mel rode into the Five Mile the afternoon tea of scones with butter and jam, fruit cake and billy tea was just finishing, the ring of a bell announcing the break was over. She could see Dev already standing outside Number One yard, talking to a few Aboriginal stockmen, all experts at their job. The atmosphere was light and good-humoured. Morale was high at Kooraki. During the ride over she'd experienced a few hairy moments she would have to tell Dev about. A dingo as big as a large dog, its yellow-brown coat merging with the ripening spinifex, had materialized out of nowhere and started following her.

Immediately she'd pulled out her whip, cracking it and swinging Gunner's head in the slouching wild dog's direction. She'd urged the bay to speed as she'd yelled at the top of her voice to the dingo, "Buzz off!" As she'd closed the gap, whip cracking, the dingo took off, running for all it was worth, its long, dark straw-coloured body flattened out like a dachshund. Mel had suddenly realized the wild dog wasn't so much shadowing her, as she had supposed, but a couple of wallabies she had spotted. The dog had obviously picked up their scent. Usually it was the dingo that struck terror into the wildlife, the cattle, especially the young calves. It was appalling, the death and destruction dingoes could wield. She had seen it all. Calves, lambs, not the Big Reds, the kangaroos well able to defend themselves, but the smaller wallabies and possums. She wasn't on the side of animal lovers on this one. Dingoes were killers. Now it was the dingo's turn. It tore off across the perfectly level plain while the wallabies got to live another day.

She was greeted with smiles, waves and doffed battered hats. She was known to all of the men, many from early childhood. Tethering Gunner, she looked up at a spectacular display overhead—a flight of a hundred and more galahs. They screeched and called to one another, flashing their lovely pink undersides as they flew overhead, swerving above and through the trees. Although she had witnessed these spectacles for most of her life, they still held her spellbound. The numbers and varieties of Outback birds were amazing: the great flocks of budgerigar, finches, parrots, black cockatoos, the sulphur-crested white cockatoos, the kookaburras and kingfishers, and that didn't include the waterfowl that turned the swamps, waterholes and lagoons into moving, jostling masses of waterbirds. The Outback was in such extraordinary good condition, so *green,* it was almost surreal—a result of Queensland's unprecedented Great Flood of early 2011. There were literally millions of wild flowers still hectically blossoming with multicoloured butterflies, bees and dragonflies floating over the vast carpets that continued on to the horizon.

As soon as Dev saw her, he came over. "Everything okay? You look a bit flushed."

"Tiny scare, not on the Tjungurra scale. I had to chase off

a fair-size dingo," she told him, as she had to. "It was going after a couple of wallabies."

"Where was this?" Dev shot back.

"Near Tarana Waterhole."

"Okay…I'll get one of the men to pick it off. I know the animal you mean. It's a cross with a runaway station dog. They're even more dangerous than the pure breed."

He turned his head for a moment, looking towards the five holding yards, then he turned his attention back to Mel. "The men have been working since dawn. They've done a great job. As you can see, they're channelling cattle from the largest yard into smaller ones, and eventually to the stock race, of course." The stock race was a narrow V-shaped alley. "We've got most of the cows and calves yarded. Halfway through the heifers and steers. No one likes mixing cows and calves with bullocks. The bulls will go into Yard Three but you won't be going near them, needless to say."

Mel nodded. She had no need of the warning. Herding the bulls was dirty, dusty, dangerous work. The alley was only the width of a beast. If it became spooked or panic-stricken, for whatever reason, it would try to charge back the way it had come, causing mayhem. The toughest hands were the ones that handled the bulls. They were the ones who wielded the stout canes, whacking any recalcitrant beast back into line. That afternoon the bulls seemed calm enough but everyone was aware of their potential danger. Many a station hand over the years had been gored, hooked or grazed in the ribs by bull rogues.

"I'd like you to partner Bluey," Dev said. "He's coming along okay. A bit erratic, over-eager, but he'll learn." Bluey was a young jackeroo, needless to say, with the nickname of Bluey, a carrot-head with an engaging face covered in big orange freckles, for all the sunblock he slapped on. She and

Bluey would be doing the lightest job. The one with least chance of injury. Mel wasn't about to argue.

"Right, Boss." She tipped a hand smartly to the brim of her akubra, thinking she probably had more expertise than Bluey, real name Daniel.

Everyone got down to business. She and Bluey worked as a team, though Mel found herself doing quite a bit of shepherding the over-eager young jackeroo. Together they were half coaxing, half pushing the remaining heifers and steers into line. Mel could see out of the corner of her eyes forty or so bulls remained to go through the alley into Holding Yard Three.

It was shortly afterwards, to Mel's instant alarm, Bluey decided to expand his horizons. For no good reason, he broke away from his job to assist a man on horseback who was wielding a whip above the head of the bad-tempered beast entering the alley. She yelled a warning to the stockman. He took immediate heed, but the tip of his whip caught the charging Bluey painfully on the left shoulder. Bluey let out a great yelp that brought forth an answering cacophony of sound from the penned cattle. However, that wasn't the problem. Bluey's yell had set off the bull next in line. With a diabolical bellow, head down, it made a butting charge at the hapless young man, hooking one of its horns through Bluey's belt.

Mel recognised, but didn't pay heed to her own danger. She felt a hot flare of fright, but she acted instinctively. Adrenalin pumping, she seized the first fallen branch that was to hand and began belting the bull's swaying rump, not slackening for an instant. The bull didn't appreciate being attacked. It gave up momentarily on Bluey. Strained horns raised to the sky, it began snorting its rage. Mel stood utterly still, none too sure she was doing the right thing, but reasoned correctly that if she made a run for it the bull would instinctively charge and overtake her before anyone could intervene.

Only someone did—someone who had the courage and expertise to handle a critical situation. Dev materialized as if by magic, moving in silence and at speed, his tall lean body moving with catlike grace. He launched himself first at Mel, flinging her out of harm's way, though the impetus sent her sprawling on the rust-red earth. Next he tackled the maddened bull, who now had Dev as his quarry. Half a dozen men were moving with stealth but alacrity to assist him. The foreman stood, rifle in hand, prepared to open fire on the valuable beast.

Only there was no need. Under different circumstances, a top-class rodeo, it would have been quite a performance that Mel would have been thrilled by, only this was present danger. She watched in a frozen panic as Dev managed to gain the enraged bull's attention. He had to be hypnotising the beast because it didn't move as he got a powerful grip on it, twisting its head and throwing it expertly to the ground.

The crisis was all but over but it left a nasty taste in everyone's mouth.

The bull safely corralled, Bluey, to everyone's amazement, walked up to Dev with a big grin on his face, his hand outstretched. "That was terrific, Boss!" he exclaimed in wholehearted admiration. "Reckon you'd win the top prize at any rodeo."

Dev ignored his hand so Bluey dropped it limply to his side.

The head stockman, with a shock of pepper-and-salt hair and a fulsome black beard, lifted his head long enough to roar an enraged, "You bloody fool, Bluey!"

Several other men added to the words of condemnation, signalling their collective disgust.

Bluey was initially stunned by this reaction, then his freckled·skin abruptly emptied of admiration. He flushed beet-red, looking young and vulnerable.

"Look at me, Daniel," Dev ordered in a steely rasp.

It was enough to cause Bluey to flinch. "Yes, sir." His red head came up.

Dev was only just barely suppressing his anger. "How long have you been on the planet?" he asked in a tightly controlled voice.

Bluey cleared his throat. He looked tremendously upset and embarrassed. It wasn't any performance to gain sympathy. Everyone could see his mortification was real. "I'm twenty-two, Boss," he said, visibly shaken.

"Twenty-two!" Dev pondered aloud. "Well, let me tell you, you mightn't live much longer if you try stunts like that again. You heard what Lew said, didn't you?" Dev's expression was grim. "What you did, your rash judgement, your inexperience could have caused Mel and you possible serious injury. Do you understand that now? I know you thought you were helping but your help wasn't needed. Mungo is well able to handle himself. *You* aren't. He really should take his stock whip to you. It might teach you a lesson."

Bluey by this time was spluttering and choking up with shame. But he was ready to take his punishment like a man. "So I'm okay with that," he mumbled, real tears standing in his blue eyes.

Dev relented. "Okay…" he snapped. "This time we'll let you off with a caution. Do the job that's allotted to you, Dan. You can support a mate, sure, but the men are far more experienced than you. You have a great deal to learn." Having delivered his verdict in a halfway forgiving tone, abruptly Dev lashed out, clipping the hapless Daniel over the ear. "Go and apologize to Mel," he ordered, "though what she did was pretty foolhardy." And brave. But he made no comment on that.

"I heard that," called Mel, accepting the foreman's helping

hand to her feet. "I had to do something, Dev," she sharply defended herself. "It could have been a disaster. Over in seconds."

"Take it easy now, lass," the foreman warned out of the side of his mouth. One look at the boss's seriously taut face had prompted the warning. It was easy to label the boss's expression. Anger. Shock. Fear. All of them combined. The foreman had been there on the terrible day when Mel's dad had been killed. The boss's fear was clearly for Mike Norton's beautiful fiery daughter. Everyone on the station knew how close they had been since they were kids. All of them had been unnerved by the young jackeroo's mindless action. None more so than the boss.

Mel was the first one to notice the blood seeping through Dev's denim shirt. She stared at the spot, then up at his face. He looked calmer now. Langdon in control.

"You're hurt?" Without waiting for an answer or his usual shrug-it-off reaction, she surged forward, unbuttoning his shirt. Nothing was going to happen to Dev on her watch. There was a nasty graze of several inches, stretching from close to the armpit across his rib cage. "Oh, that doesn't look good."

"Don't worry, Mel," he urged, a note of impatience in his voice. "I'm up to date with all my inoculations."

"I don't care," she retorted briskly. "This needs clearing up and some antiseptic applied. And don't tell me not to fuss."

"Mel, I'm not about to bleed to death," he assured her.

She clicked her tongue. "I really hate the way men are so careless with their health. And that's a sad fact."

"Not careless at all," Dev protested. "I told you all my shots are up to date."

"Then humour me," she begged. "Come back to the house.

Set my mind at rest. It's a wound and it needs washing and disinfecting, Dev. You know that."

"What about you?" His brilliant eyes moved over all he could see of her.

"A bit of a sprawl in the dust. Nothing." In fact she had skinned her right elbow.

Dev looked around at his foreman said, "Can you finish up here, Lew?"

"No problem." Lew nodded briskly. "Mel's right. You should get that cleaned up to be on the safe side, Boss."

"So you're ganging up on me." Dev gave a half smile. "Dan is off the job for today, Lew. Number Four bore is playing up. Send him out to give Sutton a hand." Not until he had given young Bluey a good talking-to, Lew thought.

He tipped his dusty wide-brimmed hat. "Will do, Boss."

"You're not going to sack him, are you, Dev?" Mel asked anxiously as they moved off.

He glanced down at her. "Hang on." He paused to remove a few dry leaves and a twig or two from her hair. "He can have a second chance. He won't get a third. That was remarkably foolish, what he did."

"Don't worry, Dev. He'll take it to heart."

"He'd better," Dev said shortly. "Don't expect me or the men to keep tabs on him, Mel. You could have been seriously injured, savaged, even mutilated. You realize that?"

"Hell, I'd say so!" she half joked, half shuddered. "But *you* were the one who put my heart in my mouth."

"So you do love me after all?" His iridescent eyes glittered with self-deprecation. "Isn't that great?"

"Let's press on," Mel said briskly. "I need to attend to that gash."

"Florence Nightingale."

"Florence Nightingale, nothing! More men died in her

hospital than on the front line. Infection, poor hygiene—life-and-death matters they weren't properly aware of at the time, sad to say. You know when she returned home she went to bed for the rest of her life?"

Dev held open the passenger door of the Jeep for her. One of the men would return Gunner to the stables. "I dare say she got around to bedside chats with family, friends and neighbours," he suggested. "I'm really impressed with the things you know, Mel."

"More like what I *don't* know," said Mel tartly.

CHAPTER NINE

THEY were back at the homestead, in the well-stocked first-aid room. "All right, you first," Dev said briskly.

"What?" Mel turned away from the large cabinet that held all sorts of dressings.

"You heard. You hurt your elbow and you're holding your arm a bit oddly."

"It's stinging, that's all," she said dismissively. It was quite tender, but then the elbow always was a sore spot.

"Let me see."

No point in arguing with him. Mel proffered her arm. Dev turned it gently so he could see her elbow. It exhibited a sore-looking red patch, a result of skinning it in her fall.

Dev manoeuvred her to the nearest sink. "I'm sorry I had to be so brutal," he said. "But there was no time to lose."

"God, Dev, you saved me from injury." She uttered a small sound of gratitude and admiration.

"So I did. I believe that puts you in debt to me for the rest of your life. Just goes to show how much I love you, Mel. I'd die for you."

Although he spoke lightly, something in his tone drew her lovely dark eyes irresistibly up to his. "I think I know that."

He gave a sceptical grunt. "You *think*?"

"All right. Expect me to die for you," she answered.

Dev watched her face. Always the magic with Mel. "That settled, I beg you to stand still while I clean this up."

"You said that like you expect me to argue," she retorted.

"Well, don't you always?" He slanted her a devastating smile.

She gave a lilting girlish laugh. Just like the old days. "I'm not going to allow you all your own way, James Devereaux Langdon. Say, would you like me to call you James from now on?"

"Don't try it." He set his chiselled jaw.

"Maybe I'd like to hear it. James…Jamie…Jimmy…Jim…" She tried variations of his given name on her tongue, only he caught her unawares.

His hand moved under her chin and his mouth came down to stop her little taunts with a hard kiss. It deepened and deepened, enough to take her breath away. Their mouths locked. Their bodies locked. Their hands locked. Eternity wouldn't be long enough.

Long minutes later, Dev hauled himself up by his strong arms to sit on the wide bench than ran the length of the room. His blood-stained shirt Mel had soaking in cold water in one of the stainless-steel sinks. The sight of his body stirred her blood—his wide shoulders, the bare bronze chest that showed off his fine physique, the hard muscle, the tapering waist, his stomach as flat as a board. Mel thought he probably had the best workout routine in the world just being what he was, the cattle baron.

"This is deeper than I first thought," she said, swabbing the long gash very gently. "But it's stopped bleeding."

Dev pretended a nonchalant yawn. "Mel, I'm not a bleeder." He wanted her to finish so he could carry her up to bed, make love to her in broad daylight. He remembered the times they had made love under a million blossoming desert stars, the constellation of the Southern Cross overhead, the galaxy of the Milky Way luminous and glittering like a river of diamonds spanning the black velvet sky.

Mel was his other half.

Mel didn't answer. She was absorbing his want. Only she had an agenda that badly needed addressing and she wouldn't be deflected. She kept busy swabbing little coagulated beads of blood from the wound. When she was done, Dev drew her body in between his long legs while Mel, from long familiarity, let her head slump against his uninjured shoulder.

"Let's go upstairs," Dev muttered into her herb and citrus-scented hair. "I want to make love to you. Love in the afternoon. How does that sound?"

Ferociously exciting. "As much pain as pleasure," she said. Despite her resolution to keep her cool, sexual hunger was blotting all else out. She touched her mouth to his bare collarbone, inhaling the scent of his skin. Emotion was flooding her. She wanted certainty, an end to all the lies. She wanted a perfect world where sordid scandals of the past couldn't intrude. Could she get it?

"Don't think I'm going to wait forever for you, Mel. I'm not a saint."

"I know that." Little shivers of excitement were racking her whole body.

"Neither are you," he whispered in her ear. Whatever he said, he knew he would wait. His intention was to make her feel unsure of him. God knew she had caused him enough pain and frustration. Frustration was a dangerous emotion. "Your room or mine?" he asked, staring into her large lustrous eyes.

Mel's husky murmur came from under her breath. "It's all the same to me."

Dev moved off the bench, slinging his arm around her. He wanted Mel all to himself. He wanted her above everything. He had taken her virginity, the two of them so young and mad with longing, struggling to hold off consummation. He would never forget their first time. He had done a lot of time-travelling over the years, reliving the whole ecstatic experience that was still, after all these years, crystal-clear in his mind. Mel was and always would be the *one* in his life. That *one* person who meant more to him than all the rest.

Dev punched in the number of Sarina Norton's luxury hotel while Mel was taking a shower. They had arrived at her apartment only twenty minutes before, after a long tiring flight. A mellifluous male voice—really should be a newsreader—told him with regret that there was no guest of that name staying at the hotel.

Dev feigned a short laugh. "*Scusi,* I should have said Signora Cavallaro." Sarina had reverted to her maiden name, it seemed.

Immediately he was put through to her room. Sarina answered after the third ring. *"Buongiorno."*

How *was* that? Sarina had invented yet another persona. *"Quanto bello!"* Dev responded in kind to Sarina's sexy opener. *"Bene in meglio,* Sarina." It did, indeed, get better and better.

Instantly Sarina switched to cool, clipped English. "Who *is* this?" she asked in the imperious tone of a dispossessed contessa. "I am expecting a call from the concierge."

"Cancel it, Sarina." Dev spoke in his normal commanding tones. "Dev Langdon here. Surely you remember me?" he asked with deep cynicism. "It happens I'm here on business, but it's imperative I have a few final words with you. This morning, if you wouldn't mind," he said with exaggerated cordiality.

Sarina took a moment to catch her breath, then her voice rose on a melodramatic note. "I thought I had answered all your questions."

"How could you have done that?" Dev challenged.

"Aaargh, Amelia has gone to you," Sarina said in a deeply wounded voice.

"You make that sound like a betrayal. Mel always comes to me, Sarina. You know that better than anyone. I've heard this riveting *new* episode in your life story. I need to establish if it's God's truth."

"So what are you going to do, sue me if it isn't?" Sarina tried the challenging approach.

"No," Dev answered coolly. "The Langdons as a family will contest the will."

No sound from the other end, then Sarina's quiet moan. *"Jesu!"*

"As a good Catholic, surely you shouldn't be taking the Lord's name in vain?"

"I *knew* you'd try it." Sarina saw herself as forever the victim.

"Not if there are no more fabrications. Mel and I intend on going to Silverton, by the way. If that's a lie, you'd better stop me now. I have precious little time to waste, Sarina, so it won't do to cross me."

"Cross *you?*" said Sarina. "I wouldn't dare."

"The only way to go."

Dev had only just put down the phone when Mel, wrapped in a pink towelling robe, walked into the living room. "Who was that?" she asked, staring across the room at him. "And don't say wrong number." Her antennae were up and working.

"You're going to insist on a name?" Dev leaned back in the leather armchair.

"You're up to something, aren't you?" she persisted, fixing him with her great dark eyes. "I know you, Dev. Just like you know me."

Dev's laugh was off-key. "Sometimes this *knowing* gets out of hand."

"You can't laugh it off, Dev. It was my mother, wasn't it?"

"*Is* your mother Signora Cavallaro?" he queried.

Mel slumped onto the couch. "Is that what she's calling herself now?"

Dev nodded. "She's a true chameleon, able to blend into whatever surroundings she finds herself in. She has a full-blown Italian accent, too. Very sexy." Dev took note of her troubled expression. "Don't let her drag your mood down. I'm here, Mel. We're together. I'm not prepared to travel to Silverton on a wild goose chase."

"You're going to see her? *Again?* You don't need to see your stockbroker?"

"I most certainly do," he clipped off. "This trip is in the nature of killing two birds with the one stone. Sarina always claimed her family settled in Sydney. We're here now. For all we know, this could be in the nature of a homecoming for her," he said acidly. "I don't trust Sarina at all. Neither do you. She's like a scriptwriter, making it up as she goes along. You can come with me if you like. Or I can see your mother alone."

Mel fired up. "She could try to seduce you."

Dev held up his hands, palms turned out. "Hey, hey, Mel, take it easy."

She fixed her pink bath robe modestly across her knees. "Sorry, but I've reached the stage where I feel my mother is capable of anything."

"Perish the thought she's capable of seducing me." Dev spoke with more than a hint of contempt in his tone.

"What's the betting, as we thought, she finds herself a rich husband?" Mel asked, thinking she would never solve the enigma that was her mother.

"One would have to feel sorry for the poor guy," Dev offered dryly. He rose to his splendid height. "I'm seeing her this afternoon. I've told her we want the final draft of the soap."

"Or you'll send some of Tjungurra's mob after her."

"Better. I'll say I brought him with me. It's all down to Sarina. I'd do anything for you, Mel."

"Anything but propose marriage again."

"That, Amelia *bella,* is the *last* thing I'm going to do," Dev confirmed. "For your sins, you're going to have to propose to me. A novel twist, but absolutely necessary."

"The miracle is you still care about me at all." She gave him a small sad smile. "Do you despise all my hangups, Dev? All the barricades I've erected?"

His expression hardened. "I despise your mother for what she did to you. Our biggest folly was ever believing her. Now, I'm going to take a quick shower. We'll dress, then go out for a leisurely lunch. After that, we'll call in on Signora Cavallaro."

Sarina greeted them at the door. She was dressed for the occasion, the very picture of European elegance. Her thick glossy hair had been recently styled in an updated, side-swept curving pageboy to just below her ears. Her deep natural wave had been straightened. She was wearing a sapphire-blue silk dress with strappy leather heels in a contrasting bright green with a matching green leather belt around her waist. To set it all off, she was wearing dazzlingly beautiful diamond and emerald earrings. They looked extremely valuable. A present—probably one of many—from Gregory Langdon, Mel thought, and stashed it away for the right moment.

Apparently Sarina had judged the time had arrived.

"Come in," she invited with cool poise, studying with approval Dev's tall, lean body and wide shoulders, the perfect clothes hanger. He was wearing a dark charcoal Armani suit with a beautiful pale blue shirt and a blue, silver and red-striped silk tie. He looked extremely handsome, reminding her of how impressive Gregory Langdon had once been.

Mel felt unnerved by her mother's pronounced Italian accent, the educated accent she had learned from the cradle and had toned down for years on end. Now it had come to the fore. "Just one question, Dev." Sarina smiled at him as though they communicated on a different level. "Why is Amelia here?"

Dev took a firm hold of Mel's hand, moving past Sarina into the deluxe hotel room. "*I'm* the one asking the questions, Sarina," he said in a clipped voice. "Let's all take a seat, shall we?"

Mel realized this was crunch time. Her mother was making a show of confidence but Mel knew better. Under the polished veneer, she was afraid of Dev. She knew he wasn't a man to mess with. Sarina, at bottom, was no fool.

"So, we're all here together *again,*" Dev said suavely. "All your fault, Sarina, because you simply won't come clean. Maybe you're incapable of it. I've heard the latest story. I need it confirmed. We're done with wading through lies. More of them and I'll commence legal action against you. You were a young, beautiful, *married* woman. My grandfather was a man with an unhappy home life. He was old enough to be your father. Seduction. Manipulation. Fortune-hunting. My grandfather's declining physical and mental health, the fact you nursed him in his last days. Telling things like that."

Mel winced. That was a powerful battery of charges.

Sarina didn't deign to look at her daughter, as though she were but a minor player. "No need to go there, Dev," she said, playing the woman of the world to the hilt.

"Give it up, Mum," Mel begged, sympathy rising irresistibly.

Sarina turned on her. "Why don't you keep out of this, Amelia? I told you the truth."

"Maybe, but it's absolutely amazing how well you can lie.

I don't know the name of my biological father, *yet.* Look on the bright side, Mum. You might be able to hold on to your fortune."

Dev broke in. "We need that all important *name,* Sarina. No problem, surely? You're big on names. Think carefully before you answer. You may have exerted influence over my grandfather, but not *me.* You have a duty to Mel to put things right."

Sarina blinked at the forcefulness of his tone. "I have your word you won't take any action against me?"

Dev gave a sardonic laugh. "I won't repeat myself, Sarina."

Sarina, the born actress, the fantasist, inventing scenario after scenario, began to speak...

As they were leaving, Dev held out his hand. "The earrings, Sarina," he said, startling Mel. "I'd like them back. They look brilliant on you, but they happen to be the Devereaux emeralds, the possession of my grandmother. They were to come to Ava. She has the necklace and the bracelet, all part of the set, but we were wondering where the earrings had got to. Now we know. My grandfather had no right to give them to you, if indeed he did."

Mel reacted with dread. Her mother couldn't possibly have stolen them. Her whole being shied away from theft.

"Of course he did!" Sarina cried, scarlet flags in her smooth olive cheeks. "I am not a common thief. Would I have worn them had I stolen them?"

"Wouldn't put it past you," said Dev, still with his hand out.

"Give them back, Mum. You'll be able to buy plenty of expensive jewellery when your money comes through."

Sarina lifted a hand to her ear. She removed the magnificent earrings with their large Colombian emeralds, then handed them over to Dev, who slid them into his inner breast pocket. "Gregory tricked me in so many ways," she said with extreme bitterness. "He swore he would marry me as soon as he was able."

Dev's tone was curt with disbelief. "I think it was more a question of self-deception. He wasn't going to marry you, Sarina. Ever."

"Like you won't marry Amelia here." Sarina threw back her head in such a way that Mel had the awful image of a taipan about to strike.

"It's eating you up, isn't it, Sarina?" Dev said smoothly. "You just can't suppress your jealousy. Even of your own daughter. Let's go, Mel," he said. "If you've held up your end of our deal, Sarina, I'll have your money released quickly. That's all you were ever going to get. *Money.*"

Back at the apartment, Mel was trying to cope with the layer upon layer of deceit and betrayal that had been allowed to accumulate over the years.

Dev, too, was very quiet. He took off his tailored jacket, then loosened his silk tie and the top button of his shirt before pulling the tie down. "I feel like a drink," he said. "What about you?"

Mel huffed. "I don't think I should go there."

"Maybe a G&T?" Dev said, walking into the galley kitchen and opening the refrigerator. He knew there were a couple of bottles of tonic inside. The gin, vodka, et cetera were in the drinks cabinet.

"The thought of any of this getting out is appalling."

"It won't come from *my* family," Dev reassured her. "They all know better. Whatever else Sarina is, she's not a complete fool. She won't talk."

"You don't think it will get into the newspapers?" Mel asked with a flare of hope.

"Is it so *terrible?*" Dev responded.

"*I* think it is. My mother manipulated everyone who got in her way. Your high-and-mighty grandfather included, it seems."

"Beautiful women have been doing that since the beginning of time," Dev said. "The great courtesans. Your mother is rarin' to go."

"La dolce vita!"

"Big time." Dev found crystal tumblers and fixed their drinks, aware of the swirling tensions between them. One wrong word from either of them and they would be in over their heads. So many fiery clashes in their time. Sometimes it was her fault. Sometimes it was his. His *mind* understood all the humiliations Mel had suffered as she'd progressed from childhood into adolescence, then adulthood. He had done everything he could to ease her pain. Only now he had to cope with a powerful opposing force. Frustration. Frustration and a lack of patience that became more and more driving as the years had passed. Mel had lacked a father and in essence a good mother to guide her. She could even be defined as an orphan, with no real sense of identity.

Well, now they knew who her biological father was. One Karl Kellerman. Kellermans were listed in the Silverton Shire's phone book. Dev had already checked it out. A list of six, including a K & R Kellerman.

Mel accepted her drink and took a long sip. "So my maternal grandparents didn't get killed in a car crash after all," she said in an emotionless voice. "And my mother's maiden name is really Antonelli, not Cavallaro. Where did she get Cavallaro from?"

"God knows!" Dev sighed, then sat down beside her. "You have living family on both sides, Mel."

"Who won't want anything to do with me."

"You don't know that. Their side of the story is probably completely different from Sarina's."

"Maybe." Mel had already considered that, given her mother's entrenched deceits. "But this Karl Kellerman—German name—didn't have much going for him in the way of honour, even common decency. No wonder my mother was all messed up. He betrayed her."

"That's for us to find out."

"At least I wasn't aborted," Mel said wretchedly.

"Don't say such a thing!" Dev reacted strongly. "Drink up, Mel."

"Drown my sorrows, you mean. I'm illegitimate," she announced as she placed the crystal glass carefully on the coffee table.

"Honestly, Mel, who cares?"

Mel turned her angry, mortified face to him. "*I* do!" she said fiercely.

Dev stood up. "Okay, you're illegitimate," he said. "Do they actually use that term these days? You were a love child. I was a love child. So was Ava and most kids."

"You're both Langdons, Dev," Mel said, straining to rein in her emotions.

Dev shook his handsome blond head. "Is this going to turn into another big angstfest, Mel?" he asked.

Don't let it be, the voice inside her head screamed in warning.

"I'm trying to deal with it, Dev, as best I can," she said in a quieter voice.

Dev grabbed hold of his jacket, shouldering into it. He was moving like a man abandoning her to her fate. "I'll leave you to the process of sorting yourself out, Mel. I don't want to say anything that might make things worse. I'm going out for a while."

"Where?" asked Mel, her back to him.

"Out," he said.

* * *

Dev didn't come back for hours. But he *did* come back. She didn't ask him where he had been. He didn't say for a good ten minutes. Then he spoke as if he had reached some juncture in his mind. "I ran into Scott Davenport."

"Oh?" Scott Davenport was one of Dev's oldest university friends. "How is he?" Mel asked. "And Frances?"

"They're both well," Dev said. "They're having a dinner party tonight. As we're in town, Scott insisted we join them. I made him ring Frances first. She said she was delighted."

Mel thought carefully. She could decline. Or she could accept the invitation. She knew this was a testing time. Maybe a make or break time for her. She was aware of the enormity of the risk she was taking with Dev. She couldn't live her life forever on the defensive. She had to make a leap of faith.

"That would be lovely," she said, trying to inject warmth into her voice. She knew that arriving on Dev's arm would be quite a talking point later for the other guests. She wondered briefly who they might be. The chic crowd, the high-flyers. Come to that, she was one herself, wasn't she? "What sort of thing should I wear?"

"Dress up," Dev said. "Not black tie, but Frances likes her dinner parties on the formal side. I have a hunch the two of them have an important announcement to make. They've been married...what?" he asked.

"Two years." Mel rose with feigned composure to her feet. A marriage wasn't fulfilled until there were children. Now, more than ever, she heard her own biological clock ticking.

CHAPTER TEN

FRANCES DAVENPORT, a real charmer, greeted them at the door, kissing them both in turn. Her golden-brown eyes shone with pleasure.

"This is a lovely surprise," she cried. "Come in. Come in. Everyone's here," she told them cheerfully. "You look *gorgeous,* Mel," she said sincerely, thinking she had never seen any other woman project such beauty and sensuality as Amelia Norton. "I was hoping to see you again. Someone here you both know—Siobhan O'Hare."

Dev didn't turn a hair. "Scott didn't say," he responded smoothly, not missing a beat.

Had Siobhan heard about Dev's trip? Mel wondered. So what could she be shopping for—a trousseau? In the world of money, power and influence, dynastic families cemented their fortunes with suitable marriages. These weren't high Victorian times and a rigid class system, but family background and money would always count.

"Siobhan? A snap decision, I gather," Frances was saying. "She has a shopping excursion in mind. I've promised to go along with her. I think you've met all the others. Annabel Corbett. Remember her, Dev?" She gave him a teasing sidelong glance.

"I do, indeed," said Dev rather dryly.

"It's okay." Frances started to laugh. "She's about to get

engaged. Now, come along." She linked arms with them. "Oh, this is going to be such a lovely evening. I know it."

The entry of Dev Langdon and Amelia Norton struck two people in the Davenports' luxurious living room with considerable force. One was Siobhan O'Hare, in her lovely hyacinth-blue chiffon dress that she had chosen with such care. The other was Annabel Corbett, who had been feeling at home and relaxed up until that very moment. Annabel was twenty-nine now, in a bit of a rush to get married. She wasn't madly in love with her soon-to-be fiancé, Bart Cameron, but Bart and his family, like hers, were old friends, well established in society. Bart would do. That was until she laid eyes on Dev Langdon again.

Annabel didn't know it, but her mouth fell open. She felt she was about to cry. Dev looked absolutely stunning—the physical attributes, that smooth, confident aura, even the walk. He was so sexy, so masculine, so golden…so…so… darn *everything*. She wanted to jump up and grab him. She knew who he was with, of course. Amelia Norton, a go-getter with Greshams, so she'd heard. It had to be said she looked drop-dead terrific in a sleekly draped cocktail dress in a rich ruby-red. Had Amelia better connections, she could have been the toast of the town. She had heard a murmur about Cattle King Gregory Langdon's will. Everyone knew Amelia Norton's mother was the Langdon *housekeeper*. She had near overheard something to do with the mother. It had been at the intermission of the opera *Carmen*. Two old ladies had been whispering behind their hands. One was Cassie Stewart. The other Valerie Devereaux. Obviously what they were discussing was hush-hush. But secrets couldn't be protected for long.

On seeing them together, Siobhan felt her every last hope had been wrecked like a yacht dashed up against perilous rocks.

Although Amelia wasn't projecting a woman-in-possession aura, Dev, on the other hand, was projecting a clear message. The exquisitely sophisticated woman on his arm was *his* woman. As far as Siobhan was concerned, there was no mistaking the signal. His grandfather dead, Dev was getting his life into swift order. Amelia had always been in his life. Now Dev was showing for the first time his adult *passion* for his childhood friend. Siobhan felt not jealous but hopelessly outclassed. Amelia was the classic Italian beauty. She couldn't compete with Amelia, no matter what she did. Neither could any other woman in the room, for that matter. She realized now that she and her mother hadn't been particularly realistic. People fell in love or they didn't. Some love affairs ended badly, others flourished. Siobhan suddenly saw things the way they really were. Life could be a messy affair.

Time now for her to move on.

Scott had chosen fine wines to go with the various delicious courses. Succulent Sydney rock oysters for starters, pâté de foie gras made in the French tradition, a choice of superb steak with either peppercorn or mushroom sauce or a classic chicken dish. A sweets trolley was to follow.

Mel sat beside Alistair Milbank, the stockbroker, feeling an easy sense of friendship and familiarity. She had come to know Alistair well. He was a close friend of her boss at Greshams, a kind, courtly man in his early sixties. He was considered absolutely loyal to his friends and very trustworthy, as he had to be in his line of work. Because he admired Mel's brain among other things, Alistair wanted to talk a little business until their host called him to order.

"Now, now, Alistair!" he warned.

"A wonderful shiraz, Scott," said Alistair, breaking off to lift his glass. Still, Alistair couldn't help asking Mel in an undertone, "Is it right what I hear?"

"What *do* you hear?" Mel whispered back, holding on to her composure.

"Your mother was left a positive fortune by Langdon?"

Mel lifted a hand of caution. "Not here, Alistair."

"I can take that as a yes, then?" Alistair asked, bushy brows raised.

"Could I ask you to keep quiet about it, Alistair?" Mel fixed him with her great dark, lustrous eyes.

A man could drown in them, Alistair thought. "Of course, love," he said, gently patting her hand. "It's really nobody's business, anyway, is it? Have I told you how absolutely breathtaking you look?"

Mel managed a smile. "Several times, Alistair. Do you mind if I ask how you came by your information?"

"If you must know, dear girl, my old Aunt Cassie. Cassie trusts me. She tells me everything. I look after her affairs now that Ed has gone. I'm just wondering how *you* would feel, if it got out into the wider domain?" Alistair looked questioningly at her.

Mel was surprised to hear herself answer with confidence. She couldn't dissociate herself from her past; it had blocked her emotional development in its way, but she could begin the process of unifying herself. She had an identity now. It wasn't the one she would have wished for, but she had a far better sense of who she was. "I can deal with it, Alistair," she said calmly.

Alistair gave a quiet chortle. "I've no doubt you can. Always thought you'd go a long way, my dear. Besides, as I say, it's nobody's business, really."

Mel nodded her agreement.

"Now, what shall we have?" Alistair was already eyeing the sumptuous sweets trolley. He took the decision making very seriously. "I do have a sweet tooth."

"Like most men." Mel smiled. She was unaware that the

tall, good-looking blonde across the table, Annabel Corbett, had never taken her eyes off them during their murmured conversation.

Had Annabel been a good lip-reader, she would have been able to make out what Alistair was saying. As it was, she had been able to catch some of Amelia Norton's murmured responses.

Keep quiet about it?

Quiet about what? There was a story there. Annabel knew she would never get it out of Alistair, but maybe Siobhan O'Hare? Siobhan was yet another one who'd had her sights set on Dev Langdon. The O'Hare cattle-and-sheep station bordered Langdon's Kooraki. If there were any juicy secrets to be told, Siobhan might know them. She had seen her stricken face when Dev and the Norton woman had walked in. Siobhan might well be in the mood to talk. She hadn't been feeling so bad of late, but tonight she couldn't take the idea of Amelia Norton landing the biggest catch in the country. When the moment presented itself she would take wee Siobhan aside.

Scott and Frances made their all-important announcement as the long, leisurely dinner drew to a close. The very slim Frances, who was not showing, was expecting their first child in six months' time. All the women gathered around to kiss and congratulate her. Dev undercut some of the overflow of sentiment with a funny joke about his friend, Scott, but everyone could see Scott was as thrilled and happy as his wife.

Annabel availed herself of the opportunity to whisk Siobhan away. "Siobhan, poppet, love your dress!" she exclaimed, barely registering it.

"Thank you." Siobhan managed a smile but she was wary of Annabel Corbett, who had been some years ahead of her at school.

"Listen, don't hold back on me," Annabel said, "but there

seems to be a lot of gossip circulating about Dev Langdon and the family."

"Like what?" Siobhan's stomach flipped but her face stayed composed.

"You tell *me*," Annabel whispered urgently. "What's with Amelia Norton, for a start? What's she doing here with Dev? She's not his sort."

"Maybe you need glasses," Siobhan suggested, thinking she could have done with a pair herself. "Amelia is very much Dev's kind of woman. Joe the goose could see that."

"Joe the goose! Who's Joe the goose?" Annabel asked in amazement.

"Just a saying." Siobhan shrugged Annabel's hand off her arm.

"Oh! I don't know much bush jargon. Have I made a big mistake, but has it got something to do with Norton's mother, the housekeeper?"

"Why are you asking *me,* Annabel?" Siobhan looked directly into the other woman's avid eyes.

Annabel appeared taken aback. "Who better? I could see how shocked you were when they walked in. *Everyone* was gawking."

"As they ought to." Siobhan gave a short laugh. "You'd have to say they make a stunning couple." Siobhan had become aware that Dev was looking keenly in their direction. His six-foot-three frame alone made him stand out from the rest.

"Couple?" Annabel sucked air back through her teeth.

"Wouldn't you say? What's it got to do with you, anyway, Annabel?" Siobhan asked. "Aren't you getting engaged?"

Realization hit Annabel that she had backed the wrong horse. "So I am," she said, affecting a one-up-on-you tone. "But how can you *not* hate the woman who must have set out to destroy any hope you had with Dev? It's not as though she's one of us."

"One of us?" Siobhan reluctantly admitted to herself that she had felt a bit like that. "You always were a terrible snob, Annabel."

"You can't be *serious?*" Annabel near shrieked.

"And hey," said Siobhan, "Dev is my friend. So is Amelia. I'd like to keep it that way. Dev was no more romantically interested in me than he was in *you.* Incidentally, if I were you I wouldn't attempt to upset him or his family with any gossip-mongering. I'd say there was probably a price to pay."

That had belatedly occurred to Annabel. "God, you're really jumping to conclusions," she hastily back-pedalled. "I only wanted a quick word."

"Well, you got it," said Siobhan. "You must excuse me, Annabel. I want to see Amelia. She looks ravishing tonight, don't you think?"

"A bit too flamboyant for my taste," snapped Annabel. She turned, rushing away. She felt furious now she'd had to *squeeze* into her figure-hugging black-and-gold sheath. So much for the cabbage diet!

Because of the strict ban on drunk driving, the dinner guests had organized Silver Service limousines to take them home. Dev and Mel were dropped off at Mel's apartment.

Everyone knows. Everyone must know, Mel's inner voice told her. She thought briefly of the morning papers and shoved the thought right out of her mind.

Que sera, sera.

Neither of them spoke in the lift beyond Dev's saying casually, "That went well. Scott has asked me to be one of the godparents."

"Lovely! I'm very happy for them both."

"Jealous?" His eyes sparkled like gems in his handsome dark golden face.

"Good grief, no."

"I know how you feel about kids, Mel," he said. "Time's slipping away."

The lift arrived at Mel's floor. "For you, too," she said tartly, stepping out. "However did you get mixed up with Annabel Corbett?"

He simply laughed. "Now that's just insane, Mel."

"I think she'd be prepared to ditch her soon-to-be fiancé if she thought she was still in with a chance."

"Then she really is nuts. Women can fancy themselves in love without giving a thought to reality," Dev said dryly. "Siobhan looked extremely pretty."

"She certainly did. You didn't know she would be in town?"

"I said so, didn't I?" Dev answered coolly, taking the key out of her hand and opening the door. "She and Annabel seemed to be having a few words at one point."

"Well, you *were* trying to give them reason," Mel said, giving him a sidelong dark glance.

"I—beg—your—pardon?"

"Their hopes must have crashed, the way you were shepherding me. I thought we'd vowed not to show how we felt in public."

"And what feeling would that be, Mel?" he said suavely, taking off his jacket and placing it over the back of a chair.

"Perhaps you wanted to give people a shock?" she suggested. "That Annabel is just so uncool."

"So she is! But think about it, Mel. Did anyone look or act shocked, outside of Siobhan and Annabel?"

The truth of that gave Mel a much needed jolt.

"Your mother taught you not to trust anyone. But you're a woman now. A woman well able to shape her own destiny. I just don't believe how you can keep putting yourself down. Alistair Milbank, among others, thinks the world of you, and I mean professionally, as well as everything else."

"Maybe going back to Kooraki, mixing with your people, has been my undoing," Mel suggested wryly. "Look, I'm going to take this dress off." She started to remove the crystal-studded barrette that held one side of her lush fall of hair behind her ear.

He could never walk away from Mel. "You look so *good* in it you should never take it off," he said. "Feel like a nightcap?"

She shook her head. "You have a big day tomorrow, don't you?"

"True," he said smoothly, loosening his tie. "What are *you* doing?"

"I'm going to start the ball rolling."

"Just as well you can't run off without me," said Dev, sighing quietly. "There won't be any big scandal, Mel," he promised. "I have people working on it. They can keep the whole thing contained."

"Can anyone ever bury scandal properly?" Mel asked.

"The best I can do is a mop up. It's already in progress," Dev assured her.

"It's not as if *I* have done anything wrong," Mel said with a rush of self-belief.

"Mel, go to bed," he said. "You're all eyes."

"I don't get a kiss good-night?" She wasn't being provocative. Dev's kisses fed body and soul.

"Well, I know I'd strive to be good, but there's a weak side to me." He smiled, getting to his feet and joining her.

"You're always there for me, aren't you, Dev?" She stared up into his jewelled eyes.

"As you might say, *l'unione fa la forza.*"

"It's true. There *is* strength in unity. I'm far luckier than I deserve, Dev," Mel said humbly.

His beautiful mouth twisted slightly as he considered what she had said. "Just remember, actions speak louder than words, Mel. We need to find our way out of this. And very soon." He bent his head to find her mouth while she leaned into him, thinking he had always put her needs before his.

Dev broke the kiss as he knew he had to. "Sleep well, *principessa.*"

The savannah lands of the north were an endless sea of emerald-green in the wake of Queensland's Great Flood. The turquoise Coral Sea, aquamarine in the shallows, lay to the east. It stretched far, far away to the horizon, its waters a maze of reefs, islands, coral banks, sandy cays and the eighth wonder of the world, the Great Barrier Reef, a continuous rampart of coral as solid as sandstone stretching north and south for nearly thirteen hundred miles. Parts of it were still uncharted, to be approached with great caution, which made Mel reflect that Captain James Cook had to be one of the greatest seamen of all time and even he had nearly met with disaster. The great French navigator Bougainville had turned back. He had written in his logbook of the sighting of a "tumultuous surf" rising out of the ocean. That could only mean a huge reef.

They landed on Maru Downs mid-morning. Dev had taken the station's long-range chopper so they could reach Silverton without recourse to a four-wheel drive. They spent an hour there, Dev talking to the outstation manager, whose wife offered tea and an assortment of cupcakes, baked ahead of their arrival. She and Mel made light conversation, but Mel could only think of two things. This was where Michael had worked as a stockman—he'd probably still be alive if, fatally, he hadn't met her mother—and next, the journey of discovery ahead of them. Mel was glad neither the manager nor his wife knew anything of Michael's story. It had all happened before their time.

Silverton, as it turned out, was one of the old gold-rush towns. Dev had sought and gained permission to land on the town's show grounds. He had no difficulty with that request. The Langdon name was enough.

At this time of year the town couldn't have looked prettier. The broad stretch of lawn in the park was densely green, the great mango trees were in blossom, crimson poincianas formed magnificent giant umbrellas against the brilliant sunlight, cascara trees laced their hanging pods with bright yellow blooms, while the ubiquitous bougainvillea climbed over every standing thing in sight.

Outside the town, a distance of a few miles, one came to the sea, with its beautiful white beaches. The beaches were lined with stands of coconut palms bent at odd angles by the prevailing trade winds, with clumps of spiky pandanus bearing their pineapple-like fruit. Mel had already discovered on that amazing resource the internet that the Kellerman Group was a family owned business established a few years before she was born. Over the twenty-plus years the business had succeeded in becoming one of the largest producers and suppliers of processed dried fruits, fruit pulps, purées and pastes to the industry.

The Kellermans must be doing well. A few years back they had built a state-of-the-art processing plant. There was even a picture of three of the company directors—Marcus Kellerman, a handsome middle-age man, with his sister, Zelma, and her husband, Bruno Campigli. Marcus and Zelma—her half-brother and -sister? They were many years older. She would soon find out if the man who had fathered her was still alive.

As for her maternal grandparents, she couldn't think they would want to see her. The horrifying charge Sarina had brought against her father remained in Mel's head like a taint, although it could be a long way from the truth. There were so many dark places in Sarina's soul.

"Sure you want to go through with this?" Dev slowed the hire car as they came into range of several very expensive-looking properties with magnificent uninterrupted views of the sea and offshore islands.

"They can only throw us out."

"I don't think so," said Dev with his built-in self-assurance. "Ah, here it is. Moongate." He brought the car to a halt outside a graceful colonial-style residence set well back in beautiful landscaped tropical grounds. "Not short of a bob of two. This property must be worth millions."

"I'm nervous, Dev."

He reached out for her trembling hand. "What did Franklin D Roosevelt say in his inaugural address? 'The only thing we have to fear is fear itself.' We're not coming out with accusations. We're on a courtesy visit. Karl Kellerman was one of your mother's teachers. Well, that's the rumour, anyway," he said with black humour. "Come along, Mel. Let's get this over with."

Mel could feel the adrenalin kick into action.

A pretty maid with a sweet smile on her face greeted them at the door.

"Who is that, Rose?" a woman's voice called.

Dev took over. "James Langdon and my fiancée, Amelia Norton," he responded by way of introduction. "Mrs Campigli?" he asked as a good-looking blonde woman, hair shot with silver, came into view. She was well dressed, a tad on the conservative side, but her whole demeanour was pleas-ant and full of self-confidence.

"That's right," she agreed. "You may go, Rose." She dis-missed the maid smilingly. "Langdon, now, there's a famous name in our part of the world."

"Gregory Langdon was my grandfather, ma'am." Dev gave her his wonderfully attractive smile.

"Well, come in, come in," Zelma Campigli invited, pink in the cheeks. "You caught me at home, for once. How may I help you? But, please, let us sit down first. Would you like cof-fee?" Eclipsed by Dev at his most charming, Zelma Campigli now transferred her smiling gaze to Mel. Now her beringed hands suddenly gripped together. "Why, I know you! You have to be an Antonelli."

Again Dev stepped in when Mel floundered. "You would remember Sarina, Mel's mother," Dev said smoothly. "She spoke of Silverton and the families she knew. We're in the region for a day or two, so we took the chance we might find you at home. I hope you don't mind. You have a very beauti-ful home. This is a beautiful part of the world."

"It is," Zelma Campigli agreed carefully, but her eyes never left Mel's face. "Just let me order coffee," she said, showing them into a large welcoming living room with a palette of coral, yellow and lime-green that took the colours from the floral print on the two large matching sofas. "Won't be a mo-ment," she said, then all but scurried away.

"We've thrown her," Mel whispered. "Or, rather, *I've* thrown her. My resemblance to my mother."

"I guess, but now we know we've come to the right town. Let's take things calmly, Mel," Dev advised. "I'm sure our talk will prove instructive."

When Zelma Campigli returned, something had altered about her face. "Obviously you'll be calling in on Sarina's mother?" she said, taking a seat on the opposite sofa. "You must have passed the Antonellis on your way here. The pinkish terracotta house with the pillars and a suggestion of Tuscany. It's only a few minutes' drive."

Dev nodded as though he knew just the house. "It didn't look like anyone was at home."

Zelma shook her head. "Adriana is bound to be there," she said quietly. "She doesn't leave the house often since she lost Frank. It was a great blow. They were inseparable, like my late mother and father. Absolutely devoted couple. You will know my father was the principal of the local High School for many years. He taught Sarina. May I ask, Amelia, how is your mother? None of us knew what happened to her. She simply went missing, like many other troubled young persons."

"You had *no* idea of her whereabouts?" Mel asked.

"As I said, my dear, no one did." Her tone was slipping a bit towards becoming condemnatory. "Frank and Adriana were devastated. You, no doubt, know the boy's death had a lot to do with it?"

Mel's heart jumped. "My mother has never talked about her past until very recently, Mrs Campigli. What boy are we talking about?"

"Oh, my dear, I'm so sorry." Zelma looked back at Mel oddly. "The Cavallaro boy. He and Sarina, fellow students, were very *close,*" she stressed. "We all remember how it was. My father called on both families to discuss the situation. They were both way too *young* to become so involved."

"How do you mean?" Mel couldn't bear to get snowed under again.

Zelma Campigli shook her handsome head. "My dear, it was all so wretchedly sad. Dino Cavallaro crashed the car that belonged to his father. He didn't even have his licence at the time. It was a miracle, my father always said, Sarina hadn't been in the car with him." Zelma's voice dropped almost to a whisper. "She was such a beautiful girl, but very headstrong. We all knew her parents were having a difficult time. They treasured her, their only child. Dino's parents were just as worried. And you knew none of this?"

Mel fell silent. Dev reached out to take her hand, keeping it in his. "Thank you for helping us get to the truth, Mrs Campigli. Mel's mother has never spoken about so many things. Obviously she couldn't come to terms with the boy's accident. He *was* her boyfriend?"

"They were violently in love," Zelma near exploded. "That was the great worry, you see. So young!" She took a deep breath, pressing back against the sofa. "May I ask where Sarina is?"

"No reason why you shouldn't know," Dev said. "She's in Sydney at the moment. She married a man called Michael Norton. He worked for us, first on Maru Downs, then on Kooraki, which you probably know is in the Channel Country in the far south-west. Mel is their child."

Zelma appeared much surprised. She blinked, then, after a moment, nodded. "You're the image of your mother, my dear. Sarina could not have wished for a more beautiful daughter." The maid hovered and Zelma beckoned to her to wheel in the trolley. Clearly Zelma wanted this extraordinary meeting to come to an end.

So many years had passed. So much sadness. Zelma couldn't imagine how any young person could have been as callous as Sarina Antonelli. But her behaviour had always been a bit on the strange side. Better not to raise the question of who was the father of her child. Her parents had been convinced that young Sarina Antonelli had been pregnant at the time of her disappearance. It now appeared that both Sarina and her child had survived.

"She didn't believe I was Michael's daughter," Mel said as they drove away.

"It makes sense, in its way," Dev mused. "The Cavallaro boy was your biological father, Mel."

"I feel sick. It makes me feel sick," Mel said. "Mum probably started lying in her childhood. It's possible she can't help it, like faulty wiring in the brain. Or she *believed* her lies. I told her once she was delusional. Her parents didn't throw her out. She did a deliberate runner. Met up somehow with Michael, manipulated him into taking her with him. Karl Kellerman was just a red herring. She named him as an act of revenge, with no regard to the morality of it. She must have blamed everyone who tried to break her and her Dino up."

Dev glanced at her with concern in his eyes. "Your grandparents were victims along with you, Mel. Your grandfather is dead, but your grandmother is still alive. We could stop off and meet her. We now know the house she lives in. Your decision, Mel. I'm with you, whatever you decide. Consign the past to the past. Or find your grandmother. Which is it to be?"

Mel's heart contracted. She smiled through a shimmering haze of tears. "We call in on my grandmother. Who knows, she might even love me."

Decades might have passed, but when Adriana Antonelli's still brilliant dark gaze fell on the young woman standing on her doorstep she reached out and gathered her into her arms.

"My granddaughter, my granddaughter!" she cried in the most wonderful, stirringly fierce voice. "Blood of my blood! Flesh of my flesh! You're here. You're really here, at last. I knew one day I would meet you. It is God's will."

Watching on, Dev knew Mel had at last found her rightful place. And at the ordained moment. He felt privileged just to be there. Mel turned from her grandmother's embrace to put her arm around him, drawing him proudly forward. Her expression was radiant...dazzling to his eyes. "This is the man

I love, *Nonna*," she said, her voice shaky with high emotion. "His name is James Devereaux Langdon." Her voice grew stronger. "We're going to be married. Very *soon!*"

"And we want more than anything for you to be at our wedding, Adriana," Dev added in princely fashion.

Adriana Antonelli expressed her great joy with a shout of laughter. "Come in! Come in!" she invited excitedly. "Do not stand at my front door. We have much to talk about."

"Amen to that," Mel murmured very softly, lifting her head to give Dev a glorious smile. "Love you."

He leaned down to her, kissed her very softly on her cushiony mouth. "Can't fight destiny," he whispered. *"We are such stuff as dreams are made on."*

There is a pattern, a meaning, a *truth* to life. One never gets to find it without going on a voyage of self-discovery—pushing every possibility for development, recognising, then containing the losses, the wounds, the fears and anxieties, the conflicts that no one can avoid in life, until, by our own striving, we reach a safe harbour.

* * * * *

CLASSIC

Harlequin *Romance*

You can find more information on upcoming Harlequin®
titles, free excerpts and more at www.Harlequin.com.

HRCNM0412

REQUEST YOUR FREE BOOKS!
2 FREE NOVELS PLUS 2 FREE GIFTS!

Harlequin

Romance

From the Heart, For the Heart

YES! Please send me 2 FREE Harlequin® Romance novels and my 2 FREE gifts (gifts are worth about $10). After receiving them, if I don't wish to receive any more books, I can return the shipping statement marked "cancel". If I don't cancel, I will receive 6 brand-new novels every month and be billed just $4.09 per book in the U.S. or $4.49 per book in Canada. That's a savings of at least 14% off the cover price! It's quite a bargain! Shipping and handling is just 50¢ per book in the U.S. and 75¢ per book in Canada.* I understand that accepting the 2 free books and gifts places me under no obligation to buy anything. I can always return a shipment and cancel at any time. Even if I never buy another book, the two free books and gifts are mine to keep forever.

116/316 HDN FESE

Name	(PLEASE PRINT)

Address	Apt. #

City	State/Prov.	Zip/Postal Code

Signature (if under 18, a parent or guardian must sign)

Mail to the Reader Service:
IN U.S.A.: P.O. Box 1867, Buffalo, NY 14240-1867
IN CANADA: P.O. Box 609, Fort Erie, Ontario L2A 5X3

Not valid for current subscribers to Harlequin Romance books.

**Are you a subscriber to Harlequin Romance books
and want to receive the larger-print edition?
Call 1-800-873-8635 or visit www.ReaderService.com.**

* Terms and prices subject to change without notice. Prices do not include applicable taxes. Sales tax applicable in N.Y. Canadian residents will be charged applicable taxes. Offer not valid in Quebec. This offer is limited to one order per household. All orders subject to credit approval. Credit or debit balances in a customer's account(s) may be offset by any other outstanding balance owed by or to the customer. Please allow 4 to 6 weeks for delivery. Offer available while quantities last.

Your Privacy—The Reader Service is committed to protecting your privacy. Our Privacy Policy is available online at www.ReaderService.com or upon request from the Reader Service.

We make a portion of our mailing list available to reputable third parties that offer products we believe may interest you. If you prefer that we not exchange your name with third parties, or if you wish to clarify or modify your communication preferences, please visit us at www.ReaderService.com/consumerschoice or write to us at Reader Service Preference Service, P.O. Box 9062, Buffalo, NY 14269. Include your complete name and address.

HRIIB

Harlequin® *Romance*

Award-winning author

DONNA ALWARD

*brings you two rough-and-tough
cowboys with hearts of gold.*

CADENCE CREEK
COWBOYS

They're the Rough Diamonds of the West

From the moment Sam Diamond turned up late to her
charity's meeting, placating everyone with a tip of his Stetson
and a lazy smile, Angela Beck knew he was trouble.

Angela is the most stubborn, beautiful woman Sam's ever met
and he'd love to still her sharp tongue with a kiss, but first
he has to get close enough to uncover the complex woman
beneath. And that's something only a real cowboy can do....

THE LAST REAL COWBOY

Available in May.

And look for Tyson Diamond's story,

THE REBEL RANCHER,

coming this June!

Stop The Press! *Crown Prince in Shock Marriage*

When Crown Prince Alessandro of Santina
proposes to paparazzi favorite Allegra Jackson
it promises to be *the* social event of the decade!

Discover all 8 stories in the scandalous
new miniseries THE SANTINA CROWN
from Harlequin Presents®!

***

Enjoy this sneak peek from Penny Jordan's
THE PRICE OF ROYAL DUTY,
book 1 in THE SANTINA CROWN *miniseries.*

"DON'T YOU THINK you're being a tad dramatic?" he
asked her in a wry voice.

"I'm not being dramatic," she defended herself. "Surely
I should have some rights as a person, a human being, some
say in my own fate, instead of having my future decided
for me by my father. To endure marriage to a man who has
simply agreed to marry me because he wants an heir, and to
whom my father has virtually auctioned me off in exchange
for a royal alliance."

"I should have thought such a marriage would suit you,
Sophia. After all, it's well documented that your own chosen lifestyle involves something very similar, when it comes
to bed hopping."

A body blow indeed, and one that drove the blood from
Sophia's face and doubled the pain in her heart. It shouldn't
matter what Ash thought of her. That was not part of her
plan. But still his denunciation of her hurt, and it wasn't one

she could defend herself against. Not without telling him far more than she wanted him to know.

"Then you thought wrong" was all she could permit herself to say. "That is not the kind of marriage I want. I can't bear the thought of this marriage." Her panic and fear were there in her voice; even she could hear it herself, so how much more obvious must it be to Ash?

She must try to stay calm. Not even to Ash could she truly explain the distaste, the loathing, the fear she had of being forced by law to give herself in a marriage bed in the most intimate way possible when… No, that was one secret that she must keep no matter what, just as she had already kept it for so long. "Please, Ash, I'm begging you for your help."

Will Ash discover Sophia's secret?
Find out in THE PRICE OF ROYAL DUTY
by
USA TODAY *bestselling author*
Penny Jordan

Book 1 of THE SANTINA CROWN miniseries
available May 2012 from Harlequin Presents®!

EXP0412

Harlequin®

American ★ Romance®

The heartwarming conclusion of

CALLAHAN Cowboys

from fan-favorite author

TINA LEONARD

With five brothers married, Jonas Callahan is under no
pressure to tie the knot. But when Sabrina McKinley
admits her bouncing baby boy is his, Jonas does
everything he can to win over the woman he's loved
for years. First the last Callahan bachelor must uncover
an important family secret…before he can take
the lovely Sabrina down the aisle!

A Callahan Wedding

**Available this May
wherever books are sold.**

www.Harlequin.com

HAR75405